"This Cir... Busine..., Rachel Told Him.

"A business is a business," Craig insisted. "I'm not going to get friendly with the ranks—it threatens the impartiality of my job."

"This isn't the marines."

Craig knew she was right. He had been acting like a drill sergeant, but he couldn't help it. He didn't know how else to act when he felt so out of place, when her close-knit crew reminded him of something he didn't have and wasn't supposed to want any longer. Even worse were his feelings for Rachel. Since his first night here, he'd been aching for her... and determined *not* to have her. But he knew full well that nothing would cool his longing for her....

Dear Reader,

Happy 1992, and welcome to Silhouette Desire! For those of you who are new readers, I must say I think you're starting the year off right—with wonderful romance. If you're a regular Desire fan, you already know what delicious stories are in store for you . . . this month *and* this year. I wish I could tell you the exciting things planned for you in 1992, but that would be giving all of my secrets away. But I will admit that it's going to be a great year.

As for January, what better way to kick off a new year of *Man of the Month* stories than with a sensuous, satisfying love story from Ann Major, *A Knight in Tarnished Armor*. And don't miss any of 1992's *Man of the Month* books, including stories written by Diana Palmer, Annette Broadrick, Dixie Browning, Sherryl Woods and Laura Leone—and that's just half of my lineup!

This month is completed with books by Barbara Boswell, Beverly Barton, Cathryn Clare, Jean Barrett and Toni Collins. They're all terrific; don't miss a single one.

And remember, don't hesitate to write and tell me what you think of the books. I'm always glad to receive reader feedback.

So go wild with Desire . . . until next month,

Lucia Macro
Senior Editor

JEAN
BARRETT

A RING OF GOLD

SILHOUETTE *Desire*®

Published by Silhouette Books New York

America's Publisher of Contemporary Romance

SILHOUETTE BOOKS
300 East 42nd St., New York, N.Y. 10017

A RING OF GOLD

ISBN: 0-373-05689-3

First Silhouette Books printing January 1992

Books by Jean Barrett

Silhouette Desire

Hot on Her Trail #574
Heat #617
A Ring of Gold #689

JEAN BARRETT

was a teacher for many years and now writes full time.
Jean and her spouse live in a Chicago suburb for nine
months of the year. Summers are spent on Wisconsin's Door Peninsula, where the couple walk the
woods and shore, collect country antiques and try to
deal as politely as possible with the annual chipmunk
invasion.

Jean keeps her readers very much in mind when she
writes her books. "The stories are for them," she says.
"If I can please them with what I write, then I've done
my job."

For Lelah and Harold, who shared the open road.

One

"**W**hen is that spy the bank's hanging around our necks supposed to get here?"

"Anytime now," Rachel Donelli answered the dour-faced man following doggedly at her heels. "And I wish you'd stop calling him that, Felix."

"It's what he is, ain't it?"

Rachel ignored him and went on with her inspection tour of the circus's backyard. Tonight was their first show of the new season and she wanted everything to be in order. It had nothing to do with the imminent arrival of Felix's "spy." It was how she would have felt about any opening performance. Well, that was what she kept telling herself, anyway.

Her energetic, long-legged stride brought her to an open cage where a rawboned youth in a sweat-stained T-shirt was speaking coaxingly to a chimpanzee.

"How's Napoleon doing?" she asked the youth. "Still off his feed?"

"Better, but he seems tired all the time. I've been trying to perk him up."

"Keep me posted, though with his condition, there isn't much I can prescribe except plenty of TLC, and he's already getting that. No, sweetheart," she murmured gently to the age-grizzled chimp who was holding out his arms toward her. "Much as I'd like to, I can't hold you right now."

"Well, ain't he?" Felix persisted, following Rachel like a determined bulldog as she moved on, stepping over the thick cables that fed power to the big top from the generator truck parked close by. "A spy?"

She refused to stop long enough to confront the man who supervised her work crew and had been with Donelli's Circus for more years than even *he* could remember. It would only encourage him. "No, Felix," she said, trying to explain to him calmly over one shoulder, although his badgering was straining a patience already stressed by her own apprehensions over their situation. "He is not a spy. He's the bank's financial troubleshooter who makes recommendations for mortgaged businesses that are in trouble. That's us, remember?"

"Yeah, and we're stuck with him. For how long, I wonder?"

"I don't know how far he'll travel with us. I suppose until he learns enough to write his report."

Felix nodded grimly. "To the bank, of course, which still makes him a spy."

"Have it your way, Felix."

They sidestepped a forklift on its way to the big top with a load of lumber for the seats. There was activity everywhere on the lot, all the preparation and nervous anticipation of the show's first day on the road.

Rachel paused to talk to the mechanic who was muttering over the automatic stake driver. "Will it last through the season, Ernie?"

"I'll do my best, Rachel, but she's old and temperamental."

"Let's hope we can afford to replace it with a new one next season." *If there is a next season.* But this was something she refused to consider.

She walked on, Felix stubbornly behind her. "This guy they're sending in to watch us, what's he know about circusing, anyhow? Probably nothing, right? Probably never had experience with anything but them high-powered corporations in St. Louis."

"I wouldn't know. I never met him. But the president of the consortium of banks he works for seems to think he has a genius for correcting all kinds of foundering businesses."

She slowed her progress to admire a young boy making tight turns on a unicycle while juggling a half dozen rainbow-colored balls. His parents were standing by to coach and encourage him. There would be many more hours of such practice for the youngster before his family considered him skilled enough to join their act in the ring.

The Rhees were acrobats, jugglers and tightwire walkers. They were also Korean. It was one of the things Rachel loved about the circus, its international flavor.

She held up thumb and forefinger in an O of approval, calling to the boy, "Looking good, Kim."

He grinned back without missing a ball.

Rachel headed in the direction of the cookhouse tent. A stately redhead rehearsing her poodles hailed her from across the lot with a cheerful, "We're gonna knock 'em dead tonight, Rachel! Guaranteed!"

"I believe it."

My people, Rachel thought warmly. They made Donelli's Circus more than just a business for her, even more than a way of life. They were her family, the only family she had ever known or wanted growing up in the circus. She was as devoted to their welfare as though they were actual blood relations. But now, as Felix insisted on reminding her, the family was threatened.

Catching up with her, he didn't know when to quit. "You realize we wouldn't be one of them foundering businesses," he grumbled through the cigar he habitually chewed, "if the weather hadn't been against us the past two seasons. All that rain that never quit kept the crowds away."

Rachel came to another stop, leaned against the side of the show's water truck and faced him with a sigh of exasperation. He glowered back at her challengingly from under the brim of the disgraceful fedora that, in the time-honored tradition of a circus boss, seldom left his balding head. Among his other duties, Felix worked the elephants because no one in the circus had just one job. He had the temperament of the elephants and a face as brown and weather-seamed as their hides, making him seem older than he was. In many ways, Rachel was closer to Felix than the others. He had been like a second father to her. A demanding one at that. At the moment, however, she longed to feed him to the big cats.

"Felix, enough. You know the weather has always been a risk and a gamble for circuses. You can't blame it alone for our situation. It's much more involved than that."

Rachel had learned exactly *how* involved late last year when she had returned from a long residence in the East, where she had been working to earn a veterinary degree, to bury her father.

Hugo Donelli's death had been a blow for her. There had been no mention in any of his infrequent letters about his deteriorating health or his mounting problems with the circus. To her dismay, she found she'd inherited a show virtually owned by a St. Louis bank and threatened by foreclosure.

Hugo had borrowed heavily and spent unwisely in her absence, his judgment impaired perhaps by his failing health. There had been exotic animals that hadn't survived, star performers who hadn't been worth their extravagant salaries and a lawsuit resulting from collapsed bleachers that insurance had only partially covered in the out-of-court settlement. No one on the show had told her about any of these things. They hadn't wanted her to worry.

The bank's president had been a close friend of her father's and a longtime circus fan. He had been sympathetic when Rachel went to see him from winter quarters in the Missouri Ozarks. He had also been straightforward.

"Is it your hope to try to take your father's place, Rachel?"

Until that moment, she hadn't been certain that was her intention. But she was suddenly decisive about it. Her career as a veterinarian would have to be put on hold. Sacrificing her circus family was simply not an option. Not when they had always been there for her, just as they were now, sharing her grief over Hugo's death. She was responsible for them. And she couldn't let Donelli's Circus, four generations old now, simply cease to exist. Not without a fight. She told the banker as much.

"All right," he'd agreed, impressed by her resolve. "You grew up in the circus. You have all the necessary knowledge and experience to take it out on the road. But the bank can't afford to go on carrying the show, Rachel. Not without certain conditions."

There had been no choice about those conditions. Either Donelli's showed a profit by the end of the year or this crucial season would be its last. There had been another stipulation—a financial troubleshooter would accompany the circus in its first weeks on the road.

"Look, Felix," she told him firmly, reasonably. "I'm as insecure about this man joining us as the rest of you on the lot. But maybe the bank is right. Maybe what we do need is an outsider's objective advice. Come on, give him a chance. *I* plan to."

Felix wasn't looking at her. His squinting eyes had shifted in the direction of the roadway at the side of the lot. His grin was slow and ominous.

"Looks like maybe you're gonna get that opportunity right now, Rachel."

She turned, following his gaze. A sporty, dark blue sedan had parked on the gravel shoulder. Both of them knew instinctively that the tall figure climbing from the driver's seat, leather briefcase in hand, was the man they were expecting.

He crossed the grassy ditch and headed their way with a long, purposeful stride. There was no hesitation in his direction, as if he recognized just who they were and exactly what he wanted from them.

"Worse than I expected," Felix growled. "What's he think this is, the executive suite?"

Rachel knew he was referring to the impeccable business suit, the black shoes polished to a flawless gloss and the erect, military bearing of the figure wearing them. They were the expressions of a man obsessive about his grooming. But there was nothing remotely effete in the pair of broad, solid shoulders that filled the blue suit like an officer's dress uniform or the narrow hips and powerful gait that indicated a virility of aggressive dimensions. He was impressive.

Their visitor's hand was extended even before he reached them. "Ms. Donelli?"

She had guessed his voice would be deep and rich, though it seemed to lack something. A mellowness? A warmth? "Yes."

"Craig Hollister. They told me you'd be expecting me."

"Yes, we are. Welcome to Donelli's Circus, Mr. Hollister."

His handshake was strong and efficient. There was no reason why the ordinary physical contact should have had her experiencing an immediate awareness of him on a level that was disturbingly provocative. But it did.

Rachel withdrew her fingers with a self-conscious haste and introduced Felix. "This is Felix Johnson, one of my bosses."

Craig shook hands with him. "Mr. Johnson."

"Just Felix," the older man instructed in his gravel voice. "Circus troupers don't have no time for formalities. We're all on a first-name basis around here."

A dry amusement hovered briefly at the corners of Craig Hollister's wide mouth, never reaching the stage of an actual smile. "I'll try to remember that." He looked toward the big top. "I was hoping to catch your matinee."

Rachel shook her head. "Not on this stand. The town is too small for two shows, which was intentional. We like to give ourselves plenty of preparation before our first performance on the road. That will come tonight. Our other dates, of course, will offer two shows daily."

"Where do you go from here?"

"We cross into Illinois tomorrow, then—"

"Your family gonna mind you going out with us, Hollister?" Felix said, interrupting Rachel. "Or won't it be long enough to miss you?"

It was Felix's cute way of trying to learn just how far the man intended to travel with them. Rachel could have smacked him.

Craig's face tightened. "I have no family," he informed them with a brusqueness that suggested this was a subject not to be discussed. Why? Rachel wondered.

"Yeah," Felix mumbled. "Well, look, why don't I get you a route sheet from the office wagon. You'll want that if you're to follow us. Let you see the whole season's schedule."

Felix's offer surprised Rachel. Whatever her urgings of a moment ago, she hadn't expected him to go out of his way to accommodate the troubleshooter. But then, she had never seen him chagrined, either.

"I'll just go and fetch one." He slipped away, making for the trailer that served as both office and ticket wagon at the front of the big top.

Left alone with the new arrival, Rachel was suddenly conscious of his formidable size. She was tall, but he topped her by at least another foot or so. She was also aware of a masculine allure in the shape of his mature face with its square, classic, male features. It wasn't a perfect face. There were deep lines around the firm mouth and a certain tension in the rugged jawline that hinted at more than life's usual allotment of stresses and burdens. Or was she being imaginative? She didn't know.

His eyes might have told her something, but they were hidden behind a pair of aviator-style sunglasses.

"What now?" he asked, a trace of wry humor in his abrupt demand. He had realized she was staring at him.

"Uh, yes. Well, since you can't see the show until tonight, maybe you'd like a quick tour of our backyard."

"That might be useful," he agreed with a brisk nod.

They began to stroll across the lot where the long trucks, along with an assortment of motor homes, were fanned out from the big top's back door like a collection of modern-day prairie schooners.

"As you can see," she pointed out, "we're not one of the big operations and it all looks like a haphazard arrangement, but I promise you there's a reason for everything being what it is and where it is. Do you know anything about circusing?"

"Next to nothing," he confessed.

She had to admit that he did seem out of place on the lot. It was more than the alien business suit and the carefully barbered hair, which under the early May sun was the arresting color of a field of ripening oats. More, too, than a complexion that lacked the tone and vigor of a healthy life spent in the outdoors. It had to do with attitude. His seemed—what? Again, she wasn't sure.

"Anyway," she said hopefully, "the bank seems to feel you have a gift for turning struggling businesses around."

"If I do," he admitted dispassionately, "it's something I acquired from my work in the marines. I had a long career of problem solving in the corps before I went into the private sector."

The marines. Maybe this explained all the spit and polish of his appearance. Also his lean physique and almost-rigid bearing. Maybe.

They moved on. She explained that most of their playing dates were dictated by towns whose various civic groups booked the show and then sponsored it with advance ticket sales and promotion. She indicated the sound truck and how it was used to advertise the circus on the streets of each community. She told him how important the condition of each playing lot was to the company and that this first rural Missouri lot was ideally flat and dry, a promising beginning.

He was observant. And he knew how to ask all the right questions. It should have been an encouraging exchange. But Rachel felt increasingly uneasy. There was something wrong here. Something definitely negative. On the surface, he was pleasant enough, but she kept sensing strained undercurrents. A certain bite to his responses, a brittleness in his manner just short of outright hostility.

She turned to him finally, searching his face, hoping to understand. She expected to catch unguarded resentment or at least an emotional detachment. She was startled by what she did read. His eyes were still veiled by the aviator sunglasses, but she could feel them watching her, appraising her in a way that was emphatically intimate. The experience was unnerving and strangely arousing at the same time.

"Something wrong?" he asked in a raspy voice.

She glanced away for a second, fighting the hot bolt of sexual excitement that licked through her insides. She was aware that Felix had rejoined them and was standing there, route sheet in hand and looking far too curious. It was the wrong moment for pursuing the situation, but she had to know.

"I think maybe there is," she said slowly. "Otherwise, why do I have this feeling that you're not exactly thrilled to be here?"

For a minute, she thought he was going to deny her impression. But he wasn't the kind of man who evaded the truth, and she respected him for that. "I'm sorry," he said directly. "I didn't think my lack of enthusiasm for this job was that obvious. Not that my opinion is in any way personal," he added in that deep timbre that stirred her senses.

Rachel struggled with her confusion. "But then what—"

"Look," he informed her with brutal honesty, "I'll be up front with you. I just don't happen to feel a small operation like yours can survive in today's world. If you were one of the giants, maybe. The truth is, Ms. Donelli—Rachel—your circus is a sentimental dinosaur in a high-tech society. I'm sorry, but that's how I see it."

She could hear Felix snorting with indignation. She didn't blame him. It was a cruel indictment. "Then why," she asked him in bewilderment, "did you accept this assignment?"

"I had no other option," he said unhesitatingly, but he didn't offer to explain this small mystery. He shook his head and went on bluntly, "That doesn't mean I'm not going to do my job while I'm here. If there are ways to put you back in the black, I'll find them. I may not know much about circusing now, but I will before I'm through, because on-site research is my specialty."

"The marines," she said weakly.

"That's right, the marines. And there's something else I can promise you. I'll be just as fair about my recommendations as I can humanly be."

Given his contempt for the circus, Rachel wondered if this was at all possible. She didn't know what to say. She resented his lofty opinion, and his position frustrated her enormously. But there was nothing she could do. The bank insisted on this man. She could only try to rescue the strained situation with a lame invitation.

"The truck over there is our cookhouse. The coffee isn't great, but it's always available." It probably wasn't the most timely occasion for introducing him to her loyal circus family, but she could see that the company was eager to meet him. While eyeing the newcomer with mounting interest, they had been slowly collecting around the picnic tables under the open-sided cookhouse tent. They were about as subtle in their intention as big brothers bunched on the front porch to check out the suspicious stranger calling on their baby sister.

Craig directed an inscrutable look toward the cookhouse tent, glanced at his watch, then wisely shook his head. "I'll take a raincheck on that. If I'm to get back here for your evening show, I need to find a motel and settle in."

She didn't blame him. It was an intimidating reception committee. "Another time, then."

"Thanks for the tour." Briefcase under his arm, he turned and headed for his car.

Felix waited until the man had started to cross the ditch at the side of the road, and then he yelled after him, "Hey, you forgot the route sheet!"

Craig looked back, distracted by Felix's call. He didn't see what was waiting for him in the long grass of the ditch. Both of his immaculate dress shoes landed squarely in the pile of elephant excrement, still steaming with freshness.

Rachel, appalled, glared at Felix. He was grinning happily. *"Felix,"* she warned him.

"Hey, it was an accident," he said, defending himself with a placid innocence. "One of the bulls must have tried to graze there when the boys were leading them down to the water a minute ago."

She didn't believe him. It had taken him a suspiciously long while to fetch the route sheet, and his shout to Craig had been too neatly timed. "No more *accidents,* Felix! And you put the word around to the others. I don't want any cute tricks pulled on this guy, whatever anyone thinks about him."

She snatched the route sheet out of Felix's hand and hurried toward the ditch. By the time she reached him, Craig had extricated himself from the sticky, foul-smelling mess. Both dress shoes were liberally plastered up and over their insteps.

Rachel watched helplessly as he tried to wipe the shoes in the grass. "I'm sorry," she apologized, choking on a sudden, insistent giggle. The look on his face really was terribly funny.

"Don't give it a second thought," he said with a double-edged matter-of-factness. "It's not the first time I've been up to my neck in—" He stopped and loudly cleared his throat. "Well, you get the point."

"Uh, you might consider a pair of boots. That's why I wear them around the lot, to protect myself from the constant mud and manure."

"Yeah, I might do that." He took the route sheet out of her hand and tucked it into the briefcase. Then he turned and went to his car. It said something about his character, the way he handled the whole thing. The violated oxfords were kicked off and dumped into the trunk. Then, in stockinged feet, with no loss of dignity, he climbed behind the wheel.

Felix had ambled over to join her. Just before he drove off, Craig saluted the older man from the open window of his car. It was a careless salute, just a hand lifted briefly to his forehead, but it was still a salute.

They watched the sedan until it was out of sight, and then Felix spat his disgust into the grass. "Just what we need! A stiff-necked ex-marine who's gonna shape up all us poor circus civilians, even though he doesn't think we're worth saving. With an attitude like that, we don't stand a chance. It's gonna be a *long* season."

When Rachel had no answer for him, he turned around and stalked off across the lot. She stood there for another minute, and then she began to saunter toward her trailer. With everything in readiness for tonight's show, the back-yard was quiet now. The disappointed crowd in the cook-house tent had drifted off, except for Buster, a diminutive clown who had more dignity outside the ring than men twice his size. A hulking brute from the work force, illogically but affectionately known as Precious, was with him, drinking coffee.

Flexing his massive biceps, Precious called out to Rachel, half teasing, half serious. "Hey, Rachel, that bank guy gives you a hard time, you know who to holler for."

It was further evidence of their caring, but she didn't need any more brotherly protection today. "Thanks, Precious, but the man was a marine. You wouldn't want to tangle with a tough marine."

Precious laughed. He didn't look impressed. Rachel moved on toward her trailer. Nearby, the dozing elephants swayed incessantly at their chains. In the direction of the bunkhouse truck, where most of the work crew rested before tonight's teardown after the performance, a radio played softly.

It was a scene steeped in tranquility. Rachel didn't share in that serenity. Her thoughts were in conflict as she reached the trailer and sank down onto the doorstep, elbows propped on her knees, chin resting on her folded hands.

She surveyed the small fleet of trucks whose blue sides proclaimed in proud orange letters: Donelli's Circus. And stretched under the name: The Greatest Little Show On Earth.

It was, too. She believed that in both mind and heart or she wouldn't be here. But for the first time since assuming control of the show, she fully understood the enormity of her responsibility and the consequences if she failed. She didn't think she could stand it if she did. Her cherished family, so real and important to her, people and animals alike, would be divided and scattered, and four generations of Donelli tradition would be gone with them.

The circus was in jeopardy, and it was maddening. Because whatever her struggles and dedication, the outcome didn't depend ultimately on her but on the decision of a St. Louis bank. And that decision would be cast on the final recommendation of its representative in the field. Craig Hollister. A husky, dynamic ex-marine whose bold look jolted her senses with an excitement she couldn't afford. And whose opinion of the circus, whatever his contradictory awareness of her womanhood, was anything but favorable.

In effect, Craig Hollister had her survival in his hands. It was a realization that scared the hell out of her.

It was after sundown when Craig emerged from his motel. The frogs were already singing in a nearby pond, and there was a chill in the air to remind him that true summer was still weeks away.

He had exchanged the business suit for slacks and a sport coat. It was as casual as he ever got on a job, even when the environment was as informal as this one. It had nothing to do with image, at least not by the usual definition. He didn't dress for success. He had read enough psychology to understand that much about himself. But his compulsive neatness wasn't easily explained, either. He supposed, in the beginning anyway, that it had to do with his origins, the lonely poverty of his childhood he had escaped by joining the marines. And then later, after the marines, when the worst happened and his perfect world collapsed around him, his careful grooming had been the result of a subliminal need to hold himself together, to cling to the only order that made any sense. Outwardly, that is, because inside him, there had been nothing but chaos. And now? Well, he guessed that now the habit was mere defense, a kind of barrier that said to people, *This is my armor. Don't try to get inside it. Don't try to get close to me because I don't know how to handle it anymore.*

He realized he was probably late for the performance as he climbed into his car and headed for the circus grounds. It was no accident. He almost hadn't gone at all. He'd spent a couple of indecisive hours in the motel struggling with the temptation to phone St. Louis and tell the bank it could get another man for the job, whatever the consequences.

It wasn't because he resented his attachment to what he regarded as a second-rate circus. He had rescued other small, struggling businesses and found the challenge rewarding. This was different. *Painfully* different. From the moment he had landed on the circus lot, he had been nervously conscious of the closeness of the unit. But the analogy in the situation hadn't really struck him until Rachel had invited him to meet the company. They'd all gathered there under the tent—noisy, cozy, genuinely caring about each other. Like a damn picnic. A *family* picnic. With his searing memories, he hadn't been able to get out of there fast enough. He couldn't travel with these people, deal with them on a daily basis. He didn't belong. He was an outsider where relationships like this were concerned. Except for those few precious, lost years, he'd always been an outsider. He had convinced himself he preferred it that way. It was safer.

But Hank Sutherland, the bank's president, had left him no alternative. In effect, Craig had been blackmailed. Either Craig accepted the circus assignment or he could take a leave of absence. Unless, of course, he wanted to quit. Which he damned well did not. There weren't many positions like this around. And his sanity would never survive a leave of absence. He needed to work. That, in the end, was why he hadn't called St. Louis.

He reached the circus grounds and was searching for a space in the crowd of parked cars when he admitted to himself he wasn't being totally honest. There was another equally strong reason why he had wanted to call St. Louis and cancel and why, perversely, he hadn't. Rachel Donelli.

Craig had spent a certain portion of his time in the motel stretched on the bed, hands pillowed behind his head as he teased himself with the memory of her. All the tantalizing, gut-tightening details. That mane of tumbled hair, a rich brown with amber highlights where the sun kissed it. The oval face with wide, green eyes, a full mouth and a smooth olive complexion. She had a pair of surprisingly strong hands and a long, robust figure clad in Western boots and a pair of trim jeans that emphasized every sexy curve. He recalled a simple shirt over the swell of her breasts and a shadow down the V of the open neck like a seductive invitation.

In the end, the soft sweetness of her femininity had Craig calling himself every fool in the book. This was bad. This was trouble.

Months after the crushing disaster that changed his life, when the worst anguish had finally diminished and he was no longer able to deny his lusty appetite, he had guiltily satisfied his physical needs with faceless, one-night stands, a series of willing partners who'd been no more interested in involvement than he was. Because involvement was unthinkable.

But with Rachel Donelli—supposing she could even sustain an interest after this afternoon's bad beginning—there would be no easy escape from a one-night stand. Not when they would be regularly thrown together, not when she was the kind of woman who could never be faceless to any man. The temptation was there. And it was *strong*. He knew from the bank's report that she was in her late twenties and unmarried. He didn't know if there was a special man in her life, but he thought not. Otherwise, she wouldn't have signaled her availability to him today. She might not have been conscious of doing it, because he sensed a certain shyness where men were concerned, but he was experienced enough to read the signs. She noticed him in a way that she didn't mean to, and he did the same.

But the temptation had to be resisted because he wasn't ready for the emotional commitment the Rachels of this world demanded. In all probability, he would never again be capable of that sort of relationship. He had had it once, it had been snatched away, and the torment had been unendurable. No, he wasn't willing to risk it.

The twilight was deepening as he left his car and headed across the circus's front yard. The souvenir and refreshment stands were brightly lighted, but there was a forlorn aspect about the midway. Few people were around. The crowd was inside the big top, the ticket wagon window closed and workmen were already taking down the menagerie tent.

Craig felt he had conquered his eagerness. But when he reached the marquee over the big top's entrance and found a stranger there, he was deeply disappointed. Somehow, he had expected to see Rachel here greeting the customers. This was an older woman, petite, with baby-soft skin and fine, blond hair streaked with silver.

"You missed the spec," she told him with a friendly smile. He looked blank, and she explained patiently. "The spectacle. The opening grand march. You missed it. The show is already into the first act.''

"Is Rachel around? I'm—''

"I know who you are. I'm Molly, Felix's wife. I'm in charge of the ticket-and-office wagon and the front door here. You'll find Rachel in the backyard.''

Dainty Molly was certainly nothing like her husband, Craig thought. One small comfort, anyway. He thanked her and found his way around the big top and into the backyard. The activity was heavy here, all the flurry of a performance underway. It amazed him to see these people, now in costume and makeup, having turned from the ordinary into the extraordinary. Even Felix Johnson, in the crimson uniform and cap of the elephant handler, looked unfamiliar as he stood guard at the back door, bullhook in hand. The elephants themselves were not yet in evidence. Craig, remembering this afternoon's experience, was grateful.

The older man glanced down meaningfully at his clean shoes as Craig joined him, then grinned wickedly. "If you're lookin' for Rachel, she's already in place for the Pete Jenkins routine.''

"Pete what?''

"Her act. Old as the hills but still gets 'em every time.''

Another surprise. Craig hadn't realized she was more than the owner and manager of the show, that she also worked in the ring with the other players.

Felix grunted at his ignorance. "Never mind. You'll see. Might as well go on in and catch the show since it's what you come for. Have to stand along the side, though. No seats left because we've got a straw house tonight. Not a bad start, is it, bank man?''

Straw house, spec, Pete Jenkins routine. The circus obviously had a language all its own. Something else for him to learn. Felix grudgingly parted the curtain for him, and Craig entered the big top where the small band was winding up the big cat act with a flourish of drums and cornets.

He found a place to stand at the front edge of the performer's entrance aisle where he would be out of the way. The cat trainer, an arrogant-looking man in glittering tights, took his applause and swept past Craig and out of the tent. While workers in orange coveralls attacked the steel arena, collapsing and removing it, Craig scanned the crowd. They seemed to be enjoying the show. All happy families, of course. He couldn't seem to escape the haunting reminder. He searched for Rachel, but he was unable to locate her.

The ringmaster, in traditional top hat and red morning coat, took up the mike in the center of the single ring, announcing with familiar, exaggerated drama, "For your pleasure, ladies and gentlemen, a demonstration in unparalleled horsemanship. Presenting the magnificent Warrior!"

Craig felt the breeze on his face as a handler rushed a sleek chestnut Arabian horse past him and on into the ring. The riderless animal circled once, head tossing majestically, and then stood patiently under the spotlights, waiting to be mounted. That didn't happen. The ringmaster looked anxious, then glanced at his watch. The crowd tittered. A prop man raced up and whispered into the ringmaster's ear. He spoke into the mike again.

"Ladies and gentlemen, I regret to inform you that our featured equestrian is unable to appear tonight. And as Warrior is far too temperamental for anyone but—"

"*I'll* ride 'im!" came the loud, gruff boast from the top level of the grandstand. "Nothin' to it!"

Heads turned, Craig's among them, to stare at the spectator who had leaped to his feet up in the last row. Craig found himself viewing a puffed up version of a country bumpkin, outrageous in baggy bib overalls, red whiskers, bushy eyebrows and a battered hat squashed over tangled hair.

"Make way for me down there! Make way! I'm comin' through!"

The intruder descended from the grandstand, pushing and stumbling through the grinning crowd. His swaggering arrival in the ring, thumbs hooked under the straps of his overalls, was greeted with boos and hisses. It was all thoroughly corny, probably no surprise to anyone in the audience, and to Craig's amazement, there wasn't anyone who didn't love it.

The ringmaster pleaded and argued with the strutting rustic, insisting Warrior was much too dangerous for anyone but the most experienced rider. Over his objections, the interloper made an awkward, bumbling effort to mount the uncooperative horse.

In spite of himself, Craig discovered he was laughing along with the others during the next several minutes as the bumpkin was bounced off the rump of the rapidly circling horse. Clinging to the tail, he was dragged around the ring, ending upside down precariously clutching the underbelly of the flying Arab.

She's good, Craig conceded. She's damned good. He could appreciate the risks involved, her expert control and careful training of the horse that the spirited routine demanded.

He watched, as fascinated as the rest at the metamorphosis that soon followed. Hat, wig, eyebrows and whiskers dropped into the sawdust from the moving horse. The clown outfit, cunningly secured with snaps and hooks, fell away in pieces to reveal the woman beneath it. She emerged radiant in a spangled costume that was skintight and very brief, permitting her a complete freedom of movement. Craig understood her strong hands now and her lithe body as she proceeded to treat her audience to a dazzling display of horsemanship. He knew he was witnessing the magic of the circus in this transformation from comic to serious. But he couldn't have described a single one of the superb feats she and her mount executed in the next seven minutes. He was aware of nothing but the hot lights bathing her smooth flesh and of his own arousal. He wondered if every man out there was experiencing the same desire for her. With a sudden, irrational jealousy, he resented the sea of male eyes feasting on her, was angry with her because she dared to expose herself in that scanty outfit to anyone but him. He was crazy.

His dazed brain vaguely registered a storm of applause and a blurred awareness of the handler leading the sleek animal past him and out of the tent. Then Rachel, smiling her appreciation, hand lifted in farewell, left the ring and started up the shadowy aisle. He moved, stepping into her path. She saw him and stopped. They stood there, only inches apart now, gazing at each other, not moving, not speaking.

Despite the hundreds around them, Craig felt as if they were suddenly alone in a hushed, canvas world. He couldn't have said what act was now performing in the ring. Clowns, elephants, acrobats. He didn't know. He was conscious only of her. Of her hair drawn back from her incredible face and fastened in a snug twist at the nape of her neck. Of a tiny scar at the corner of her full, slightly parted mouth. Of the pulse beating in the hollow of her throat. There was a fine sheen of perspiration on her skin, her breasts rising and falling from her recent exertions in the ring. It was a tantalizing business that left a tightness in his chest, a rawness in his throat.

Rachel was accustomed to men staring at her nightly in the ring and thought nothing of it. But this was different. This was breath robbing and hotly intimate, like a naked embrace.

She had been startled to find him standing here. Now she was startled by the pair of eyes the sunglasses had earlier hidden from her. They were the stunning blue of a deep lake. And they were fierce with emotion. There was a clear male arousal in them that shocked her in its intensity. And then slowly, emerging from behind careful barriers, came a vulnerability she didn't understand. An actual flash of bleakness quickly replaced by smouldering anger. He was angry with *her,* blaming her for this sexual tension that was sizzling between them.

Craig knew he was being unreasonable. He couldn't help it. He did resent her for awakening in him something he wasn't able to confront. Something that he hated because a potential suffering lurked behind such feelings, and he'd had his share of that. Enough to last him a lifetime.

He had to get out of this. He had to rescue the moment and then see to it that it was never repeated. Whatever it took, he had to avoid being near her like this in the future. He'd never survive otherwise.

His voice was husky but dispassionate enough when he told her, ''I liked your act.''

''Thank you.''

''You're welcome.''

And that was all. It was enough. He turned around and managed to get out of the tent. He didn't pause, and he didn't look back.

Two

On Tuesday, at their stand in Murphysboro, Illinois, the cat trainer stormed into Rachel's trailer, his handsome face flushed with indignation. "This bank man is demanding to know why I have to feed my Bengals such expensive cuts of meat! The tigers won't know the difference, *he* says! He has read up on it, *he* says! What does he want me to do? Give my lovely babies a diet of midway hot dogs?"

On Thursday, in Evansville, Indiana, one of the work crew came to Rachel, his expression mutinous. "That character from the bank is on my tail every minute! Following me around askin' questions, why this, why that! Jeez, he's even pestering me about the damned portable toilets! He keeps on my case like this, Rachel, I'm blowin' the show!"

On Friday, back in Illinois, Molly Johnson, always amiable with everyone, cornered Rachel in the office wagon. "Rachel, he's been in here poking through all the records. Not just the financial statements and route books. I know he's entitled to see those. But the personnel files! The *con-*

fidential personnel files! I tried to tell him, but all he did was ignore me.''

The cook came to Rachel. His helper came to her. The man in charge of the spool truck that wound and carried the canvas came to her. By the end of their first week on the road, it seemed to Rachel that there wasn't a member of the company who hadn't some complaint for her on the subject of Craig Hollister. Remarkably, Felix was not among them. She understood why. The belligerent Felix refused to acknowledge his enemy on even these terms.

Rachel handled each grievance in the same manner. She made soothing sounds. She advised patience. She reminded everyone that the survival of Donelli's Circus depended on their cooperation. And privately, quietly, she went out of her mind.

She knew she ought to go to Craig, talk to him about his high-handed methods with her people. But she resisted that course of action and was afraid to admit to herself the explanation for her reluctance. Anyway, since the first night in the big top, Craig had been deliberately avoiding her. Not an easy thing to manage in the intimate environment of a small circus, but he somehow achieved it. She heard about him constantly, but she rarely saw him, and then, never alone. It didn't seem to matter. Even at a distance, she was aware of his compelling presence and the crackling tension he created whenever he was on the lot.

There was no point in denying it. She *was* strongly attracted to the man. But feeling as he did about the circus, which was her whole life these days, it would be a mistake to involve herself with him on any personal level. He must realize this himself. Why else would he be so conspicuously keeping out of her way? It was probably a wise measure. But she wasn't happy about it, and she wondered how they were going to withstand each other in the long days ahead.

Rachel could no longer evade the situation when, pitched next door to a stopping center in Decatur, Illinois, her lanky ringmaster and performance director, Ray Ford, came to her.

"Rachel, you're going to have to do something about this guy. He's getting in everyone's hair. We all understand why he has to be here and what he has to do. It's his *way* of doing it. Rushing us like he can't wait to get the job finished so he can get faraway from all of us. He's growly about it, too. Acts like some testy sailor who's been at sea for too many weeks and is taking his frustration out on his mates. If you get what I mean."

Rachel was afraid she did. After that riveting experience with Craig on opening night, she was very much on edge herself these days. "All right," she sighed, "what's he done now?"

"Go and see for yourself. He's in the big top with a measuring tape. He's trying to prove we can fit two rings in there instead of one and then add more seats. All in the same space, mind you. Says it will increase the show's revenue. I tried to tell him just why it's not possible, but as usual, he's not listening. Rachel—"

"I know, I know. I'll talk to him, Ray."

"Well, before you do, there's something else you ought to know. I get the strong feeling when I'm around this guy that his attitude about us isn't just because he doesn't approve of the circus as an industry. I think it's more complicated and personal than that."

"What do you mean?"

Ray's thin face was thoughtful. "I don't know. It's like he's bothered by the closeness of the company, even the families that attend the show. But at the same time he's resenting us, he'd like nothing better than to be a part of us. You know, like the miserable kid who hasn't been invited to the party and swears he doesn't care when, underneath, he really does."

Ray could be very insightful about people, but Rachel doubted his opinion this time. Craig might be resisting any close association with her, probably with good reason. But he didn't strike her as a man who was confused about his needs, just as someone who was self-contained and preferred it that way. Whatever the explanation, she wasn't looking forward to confronting him as she left her ringmaster in the cookhouse tent and headed toward the big top. The problem had to be resolved, but she feared Craig's reaction might be unpleasant.

All the others were at lunch before the matinee. The tent was deserted when she pushed through the back-door curtain, stopping just inside the entrance to adjust her eyes to the muted light. She never failed to experience the warm benediction of the big top when it was like this, hushed, soothing in its peaceful gloom, like a great canvas womb.

She saw him at once. Tape in hand, he was pacing off the length of the playing area, head lowered in a frown of concentration. He paused, head still down. A shaft of daylight, finding its way through the opening around one of the center poles, pinned him in its glow, turning his thick hair into molten gold. Rachel caught her breath. She was nervous enough over this showdown without finding him this way, standing there like some potent sun god.

Steeling herself to the inevitable, she started toward him. He became aware of her then. His head shot up. To her surprise, his chiseled face wore a look of eager pleasure that tugged sharply at her emotions. It was a mutual recognition of what they had both been silently feeling. Then as she approached him, his expression instantly became something else. Alert, defensive.

"You want to see me?" His deep voice was wary. He wasn't happy that they were alone here together.

"Yes."

"About my idea for two rings in here, I suppose."

"Among other things."

"Well, don't worry. I've decided the plan probably isn't practical, though I felt if you were to reduce ring size and squeeze in two—you know, multiple acts playing simultaneously like the bigger circuses—it could measurably increase your gates.''

She tried to explain the situation to him with a nonchalant tolerance, not easy when his forceful nearness had a heated impact on her senses. ''Craig, all circus rings, whatever the size of a show, are always forty-two feet in diameter. Never more and certainly never less. It permits the necessary centrifugal force for the riding acts.''

''Oh, I didn't know.'' He nodded thoughtfully, and then his blue eyes narrowed. ''What other things?''

''You and I have a problem, I'm afraid.''

He looked cautious again, stiffening slightly. No, she pleaded to him silently, not *that* problem.

''Uh, look,'' she suggested, ''can we sit down for this? I think we need to talk.''

He hesitated, then led the way to the nearby bleacher section. Rachel settled on the bottom tier. Craig perched on the step above her and to her right, as though not trusting himself to be on the same level with her.

He faced her, ready to listen. ''All right, what is it?''

She decided to be direct. ''It's—well, it's your attitude. I don't know if you realize it, but you're alienating the whole company.''

He stared at her, his gaze hardening. He didn't look in any way surprised. ''They've been complaining to you, I suppose. They resent the interference of an outsider. Don't worry, I'm used to it. It's happened before when I've had to go in and troubleshoot a business. They'll get over it.''

She shook her head. ''No, you don't understand. The circus isn't like other businesses. We can't be measured in those terms.''

''A business is a business,'' he insisted. ''They all have certain traits in common. That's my specialty, remember? And I don't get familiar with the ranks because it threatens the essential impartiality of my job.''

He was making her angry. "How can you perform that job when people won't cooperate? And they're not going to cooperate if you won't at least be diplomatic with them."

"I am being diplomatic."

"No, you're not. You've been acting like this is the marines and we're all being court martialed, with you the prosecuting officer. You—you're not being *human*."

Rachel regretted that last word the instant it was out of her mouth and she saw his reaction. He went rigid where he sat and his face wore the same obscure bleakness she had recognized on the day he had joined them. Could Ray be right? Was Craig, in fact, a lonely man needing something he strenuously denied in himself? Whatever the reason for his distress, it moved her deeply, though she didn't think he'd appreciate her sympathy.

Expecting a hostile response out of him, she was surprised when he said quietly, "What would you suggest?"

She tried to be gentle this time. Understanding him a little better as she now did, she felt he deserved that. "You could start by not wearing that suit and tie all the time."

He actually smiled at that. "My marine-style uniform, you mean."

"Well, a more casual look would help, I think. A circus lot isn't exactly a corporate headquarters."

"And?"

"You don't have to get familiar with the company, but at least you could try to relax around them so they can begin to trust you. As it is now..."

She didn't need to say more. She knew he got the point. He was thoughtfully silent for a long moment as she watched him, waiting for his decision. She could see he was struggling with himself.

Craig knew she was right. He *had* been behaving like a drill sergeant. He couldn't help it. He didn't know how else to act when he felt so uncomfortably out of place here, when every awkward minute he was with these people, they reminded him of something he didn't have and wasn't supposed to want any longer. Even worse were his frustrated yearnings for Rachel. He wondered what she would say if he told her that she, too, was responsible for his aggressiveness with her circus family. Would she be shocked to learn that, since his first night here in the big top, he had been aching for her while perversely determined not to have her? That this also accounted for his gruffness?

Shifting himself uneasily on the bleacher where he sat, he faced another truth. His efforts to avoid her weren't working. He still wanted her. Distance didn't help. Even if he left the circus and went back to St. Louis, it probably wouldn't cool his longing. There was no use then in keeping away from her. So what was he supposed to do?

He thought about it for a few seconds, feeling helpless, and then he reached a decision. It was pointless to go on fighting this thing. Maybe it was time he gave it a chance, learned if it was real and if he could handle it. But how was he going to do that? How was he going to initiate any closeness with her when he wasn't sure she would be receptive after all his deliberate remoteness?

Then he had an inspiration. He remembered something Molly had been telling him before he'd managed to earn her unfriendliness in the office wagon. She had described a place he ought to visit if he really wanted to understand the circus. He didn't understand the circus or appreciate it. He had always prided himself on his thoroughness in his work, but out of resentment and a failure to investigate resources, he had neglected his homework with this assignment. His ignorance about ring size was proof of that. He needed to remedy this.

Rachel was surprised when Craig slid down from the bleacher above her, closing the distance between them as he joined her on her level. She was even more surprised by the husky challenge in his voice. "All right, but you'll have to show me how."

"Show you—what?"

"How to relax."

His sudden nearness was unsettling. She laughed. A small, nervous laugh. "You're not serious."

"Yeah, I am," he promised her solemnly. "I've forgotten how to relax, Rachel." More than that, he told himself regretfully, he had forgotten how to *feel*.

Craig didn't offer to explain his baffling declaration, but she knew he meant it. She shook her head helplessly. "And just how do I—"

"There's someplace I have to go. I'd like to combine business with pleasure when I go there, make it a day's outing. Come with me," he urged. "Teach me how to relax, Rachel."

"You're crazy. I can't just pick up and leave the circus."

"Yes, you can. For this one day, you can. The show isn't scheduled to play on Sunday. We'll be sitting on a lot up in eastern Iowa then, within driving distance of where I need to go."

"Where? What place?"

His smile was slow, mystifying and very persuasive. "I don't think I'll tell you. I think I'll keep it a secret. Maybe that way, you won't be able to resist."

"But—"

"Say yes," he commanded.

He was right. She wasn't able to resist. But it had nothing to do with his mysterious destination. She was surrendering to a male voice rough with surprising eagerness, and a teasing, blue-eyed grin that turned her insides to a defenseless jelly.

"Yes," she softly agreed.

Rachel's simple yes had the most astonishing effect on the atmosphere of Donelli's Circus. Its members may not have been able to explain the change, but they did know that something remarkable had happened. Why else was Craig

Hollister so suddenly, miraculously cheerful with them? The guy was practically whistling as he strode around the lot. They didn't question it. They just welcomed it with relief and went about their work with grateful smiles.

Most of them were asleep in their trailers, glad of a rare free day, when Craig arrived from his motel early Sunday morning to collect Rachel. She was amazed at his appearance when she joined him in his car. He was wearing snug jeans, an open-necked polo shirt and tennis shoes. He looked unfamiliar and thoroughly sexy.

"What?" he asked innocently as she turned to stare at him.

She shook her head. "Nothing." True, the tennis shoes were a pristine white, the jeans unfaded and the polo shirt without a blemish, but it was a beginning. "I was just wondering whether I get to know where we're going."

"Not yet," he said, refusing to disclose their destination as he turned out of the lot and headed for the highway.

Rachel didn't press it. She was much too sleepy. Yesterday's haul from central Illinois had been a long one, putting them on the new lot in Iowa at a late hour. Covering a yawn, she settled back in her seat and promptly drifted off.

The sun was high when she wakened to find them traveling through wooded hills and green farmland. "Where are we?"

"Wisconsin."

"Where in Wisconsin?" she demanded.

"You'll see."

Maddening, she thought, and she began to look for clues in the road signs they passed. It was several minutes later, as they neared his objective, that Rachel finally understood. "Baraboo! The Circus World Museum at Baraboo!"

He turned his head to grin at her engagingly. "Molly said you hadn't been here since you were a girl and that she didn't think it would be redundant. Okay?"

"Better than okay. When it's in the blood, you can never get enough of the circus." Rachel was touched by his surprise and delighted by the opportunity to revisit a place that was sacred to circus troupers.

"I thought it was time I got an overall picture of the industry," Craig said.

When they reached it, he discovered that the open-air museum offered him just that and much more. Located along the banks of the Baraboo River on the site of the Ringling brothers' original winter headquarters, the place was fascinating. The research library was closed on Sundays, but that didn't matter when there was so much else to see. The history of the circus had been lovingly preserved on the compact grounds.

In one of the exhibition buildings, they marveled over a complete, working miniature of the Ringling's show in its golden years. In another building, they viewed the vast collection of restored parade wagons. Outdoors, they watched a street parade and a demonstration of old-time circus-train loading.

The crowds everywhere testified to the interest the American public still had in an entertainment that was as old as their country. Craig also found them an excuse for holding Rachel's hand. "Just so you don't get lost," he claimed, his expression perfectly sober, though his mischievous gaze suggested something else.

Rachel didn't object. His big, square hand clasped protectively around hers may not have been necessary, might even have been hazardous, but it was warmly satisfying. It also made her acutely aware of the sensual excitement that had been strumming between them all day.

More than that, she simply enjoyed being with him, pleased to see that he could put aside whatever private cares troubled him and relax in her company. He had revealed a sense of humor before this, but it had been a grim, forced kind of amusement. This was something else, carefree, boyish. She delighted in his hearty laughter over the antics of a chimp act during the performance in the big top erected at one end of the grounds. He became another man when he laughed, one who almost stunned her with his appeal.

Craig was careful not to mention that the act reminded him of the lone chimp kept in its own spacious cage in Donelli's backyard. The animal was neither displayed nor worked, a needless expense he had yet to understand. But he didn't want to mar the day with the problems of Rachel's circus. All he wanted to do was watch her lovely face being mesmerized by the performance. She was like one of the exuberant kids in the audience, and it astonished him that she could be so engrossed when she lived with the circus daily.

He knew she was comparing the performance to the Donelli production and finding her own show equally entertaining. Afterward, she dragged him around to the back door to talk briefly to the players. It was not surprising that she knew most of them. He had already learned the circus community was a clannish one. It was irrational of him to mind when they greeted her so warmly, trading precious memories from the days when some of them had trouped on the Donelli show. They were friendly enough when Rachel introduced him, but he knew they regarded him as an outsider. He couldn't help it. He felt that old ache of being excluded from something intimate and special.

"What's wrong?" she asked him when they were alone again.

"Nothing.... Yeah," he grumbled, snatching at a valid excuse for his sudden glumness, "the bareback rider. She was practically spilling out of her costume. Why do those outfits have to be so skimpy?"

Rachel laughed. "Craig, you're a prude!"

He wasn't. He didn't care if the woman paraded naked in the ring. What he had been trying to tell Rachel was that he minded her own brief costume that first night when he could

have strangled every male in the audience who was captivated by her supple body. He was stupidly jealous of a
woman he had never even kissed and barely knew. But he
planned to remedy that.

"Come on," he urged, shaking off his mood. "I'm
starving."

She was hungry, too. It was nearly midafternoon, and
though there were refreshment stands all over the park, he
had said he hadn't wanted her to spoil the lunch he was
planning for them.

His strong hand had possessively claimed hers again, and
he was drawing her toward a bench near the elephant rides.
"Where are we going?" she asked. "Aren't we going to
leave here and find a restaurant?"

"You wait right there on the bench," he directed. "I
won't be five minutes."

What now? she wondered.

When he returned from the parking lot, he was bearing a
picnic cooler. "Where did that come from?"

"It was in the trunk," he said. "I put it together last
night. What do you think?"

"As long as there aren't hot dogs, cotton candy and pop-
corn in there, I'm impressed."

She discovered to her pleasure moments later that the
cooler contained offerings far more imaginative than that.
They found a secluded picnic table screened by weeping
willows along the edge of the river. When they had settled
side by side on the seat facing the lazy, sun-dappled waters,
Craig unpacked a spread of delicacies ranging from smoked
salmon and imported cheese to fresh California strawberries.

"Now I *am* impressed!"

"Listen," he boasted playfully, pouring them glasses of
zinfandel, "when it counts, we marines know how to do it
in style."

Rachel appreciated his creative effort, though she suspected he might personally have preferred cold beer and ham sandwiches. He handed her one of the glasses of wine, and she sipped contentedly as she gazed at the burbling river. "Mmm, this is nice. The setting, all of it."

"The best part of it is," he said, opening a package of crackers, "we don't have the Donelli clan looking over our shoulders."

She chuckled in understanding. "They are a bit paternal about me, aren't they. It's because I grew up in the circus, and a lot of them were there helping me as I did."

"You had your father, didn't you?"

"Yes, but no one else. My mother died when I was a baby, so— Here, let me do that." She took over filling a paper plate with crackers and rolls. "Anyway," she went on, "they helped Dad to raise me. Felix was there watching me take my first steps. Molly taught me my letters and saw to it that I didn't neglect my school lessons. Lucille—she's the poodle act—shared the excitement of my first boyfriend and then cried with me when he dumped me. And Precious— big, tough Precious—sat up with me all night when I was miserable with the mumps. Are there napkins?"

"Here." Craig passed a package of napkins to her.

"They've always been there for me," she continued, removing a pair of napkins. "They did everything brothers and sisters and cousins and uncles and aunts are supposed to do, and more. What can I say? They're my family, all of them." She smiled softly over the memories. "Well, you know what family bonds are like."

He didn't say anything. She glanced at him and was startled by the lost, hungry look in his eyes, an expression of poignant yearning that troubled her deeply. "Craig?"

For a moment, she didn't think he was going to answer her. Then in a voice hoarse with restrained emotion he said slowly, "No, actually, I don't know much about family bonds. I never knew my mother or father or anything about

them. I was abandoned when I was two months old.'' He
laughed dryly. ''Would you believe in a tavern? There was
a series of foster homes after that, some of them good, some
of them not so good.''

''You—you weren't—''

''Abused? No, never anything like that.''

''But you weren't nurtured, either, were you?'' she
guessed.

He shrugged and she could see that he regretted telling her
anything at all, that he regarded his lapse as a weakness. ''I
had the marines when I was old enough. They gave me a
further education, taught me how to be independent and
rely on myself. It was all I wanted or needed.''

No, Rachel thought sadly, it couldn't have been enough.
But she had to let the subject go because Craig was clearly
not willing to discuss it anymore.

''Everything's ready here, isn't it?'' he asked impatiently. ''Let's eat.''

In the next several minutes they were silently busy satisfying their appetites. Then between bites, Craig shared an
observation with her. ''I watched your face during the show.
You were so caught up in it all. The circus really does mean
everything to you, doesn't it?'' It was a realization that
suddenly bothered him, but he didn't tell her that.

Rachel shook her head, swallowed a mouthful of salmon,
then tried to explain it to him. ''Not everything, I hope, but
it does matter a lot. I guess by now you must think all circus troupers are a little crazy. I suppose we have to be to put
up with all the mud, sweat and tears that come with haul-
ing all over the map. But, you see, I happen to feel it's worth
it for those few hours of wholesome excitement we can bring
to families in small towns that rarely get live shows.''

She paused, spreading pâté on a cracker while she gathered her thoughts. ''Maybe all that sounds a bit corny in this
cynical age of passive, electronic entertainment, but I'm
convinced that a traditional show like ours still has real

value. Not just the nostalgic side of it, either. It's because there's an intimacy about the one-ring circus that involves the audience on a personal level. That's not possible at the bigger shows." She laughed. "Do I sound like a woman with a cause?"

"No," he said gravely, "you sound like a woman committed to something she loves." A strong, vital woman that he very much admired, though her devotion to the circus still bothered him. Maybe it was because he feared she could have no room for anything else in her life. And if that was so...

"Rachel," he asked suddenly, "what will you do if your show doesn't make it, if in spite of everything, it has to fold?"

"I refuse to let myself think about it," she said simply, biting into the cracker.

He applauded her spirit, but he felt she was being unrealistic. "But it can't be your whole life. What about that half of the year the circus isn't on the road?"

"Well—" she paused to chew the cracker "—there's a lot to do over the winter to prepare a show for its new season. Also, I'm hoping to get my Missouri license so I can begin practicing veterinary medicine out of winter quarters."

He was surprised and impressed. "I didn't realize you were a qualified vet. How did that happen?"

"Rudy Mueller."

She said the name casually enough, but Craig's instincts told him this was someone who had been important in her life. Maybe someone for him to worry about. "So, who was this Rudy Mueller?"

"A star equestrian Dad imported from Germany for one of our seasons. He was a brilliant performer. He could do things with a horse that took your breath away. Anyway, he took *my* breath away."

"Serious?"

"Serious enough, though I'm not sure now whether I was in love with Rudy himself or his genius in the ring. Either way, I was devastated when he left the show. He'd neglected to tell me there was someone else waiting back in Germany."

"Bad time?"

"It would have been," she said, reaching for the strawberries, "if my circus family had permitted it. See, I'd had this longing to be a vet ever since I was a kid. I suppose it was natural, growing up on the show with all the animals, loving them as I did. Only I never did anything about my ambition. After high school, I went on performing my riding act with the show. Just letting myself drift, I guess."

"Until Rudy."

"Right. My family gave me no time to suffer over him. They insisted I put him behind me and get on with being a vet. Which," she said, dipping a fat strawberry into a container of powdered sugar, "is what I did."

Rachel paused again to chew on the sugar-coated strawberry before continuing. "It wasn't easy. I was out East all those years. The training was long and hard, and I missed the circus and all my friends. Dad encouraged me to stick with it, and I did. I was so busy applying myself that I hardly ever got home, and when I did, the visits were short ones."

She reached for another strawberry. "The worst of it was," she confided, "I lost touch with the show. I never realized until after Dad died that the circus was in financial trouble. I suppose he and the others kept it from me because they were afraid if I knew, I'd leave school and come home to help out."

"Which is what you have done," Craig pointed out.

"Yes, but I did complete my training, so maybe one day..." She ate the second strawberry, urging the dish on Craig. "Mmm, try one. They're great."

He shook his head. He wasn't interested in strawberries. Now that he had satisfied his need to know about her, he was impatient to please another appetite. The opportunity was as ripe as the fruit.

There was a smear of powdered sugar at the corner of her mouth. He leaned forward, his forefinger slowly wiping away the sticky sweetness. It was a casual gesture, but to Rachel, it felt like a warm caress.

Their gazes collided, his a vivid, smoldering blue; hers, startled and questioning. His explanation was easy and innocent, but his voice was so low and rusty when he spoke the words that she trembled.

"You had some powdered sugar there. See?" He held up the finger with the dab of white on its tip. While she watched, her eyes widening, he slowly licked the sugar from his finger. It was a sensual gesture, as though he were tasting her.

"Craig—"

"Wait." His finger, still damp, came back to her mouth, brushing gently just above the corner.

"More sugar?" she murmured, her mouth suddenly dry.

"No. There's a little scar here. I've been intrigued by it since that first day."

"Oh. It—it's a souvenir from a fall I took when I was twelve."

"Horse?"

"Mmm."

His finger didn't go away. It lingered there, softly tracing the outline of the almost invisible scar. Then the finger drifted to her mouth, lazily exploring the contours of her lips. It was a voluptuous mouth, he thought, as provocative as her dewy, green eyes with their sooty lashes. Those green eyes watched him nervously. But she didn't object, and he could feel her pulsing under his touch.

"Satisfied?" she whispered.

"Not yet," he said, his face closing on hers.

Her heart kicked as his mouth found hers. He caught her lower lip, sucking on it gently. Then the point of his tongue trailed across her upper lip, leisurely tracking what his finger had investigated. He whispered small kisses around both her lips while her senses clamored under his maddening restraint.

Only when she squirmed with visible impatience did his parted mouth settle firmly against hers. And what had been unhurried and teasing became quick and eager, a flaring incandescence as he deepened the kiss, his searing tongue mating with hers.

Craig's senses rioted on him. She tasted of strawberries, sweet and succulent, her mouth warm, enticing. He could feel a hot, heavy thickening in his loins as he went on kissing her, his fingers tangled in the masses of her sunburnished hair.

When the last air had been robbed from him, he lifted his mouth reluctantly from hers, resting his forehead weakly against her brow.

Her voice was shaky when she asked him, "Is this another example of how the marines do it in style?"

He smiled happily. "What do you think?"

"I—I'm not sure," she said in a small voice. "Could we try it again?"

She was greedy for him. He liked that. Hell, he loved it. He didn't hesitate to oblige her. This time, with their bodies twisted around on the seat to better accommodate each other, he was able to hold her properly. Her body snugged against his, a perfect fit. Tenderness deserted him, a raw passion flaming between them as his mouth sloped eagerly across hers in another searing kiss. The blood surged through his vitals until he ached with his arousal.

His arms tightened around her. He could feel the heat of her lush breasts pressed to his chest, could tell that her nipples were puckering for him through the thin material of her shirt. He went wild with the urge to reach up between their bodies and fill his hands with their softness. Sensitive to the time and place, he made a great effort to resist. Lord, he wished they were somewhere alone and private, anywhere but out here at a public picnic table.

Rachel, too, must have realized their situation. She finally leaned away from him with a small, quivering laugh. "I think maybe it's time we packed up and got out of here before someone reports us for lewd conduct."

"Give me a minute," he pleaded, adjusting his jeans over his still painful arousal.

She was kind enough not to laugh again. She got up and began loading the cooler. He wished she wasn't so suddenly casual about what had happened. He watched her, groaning softly with frustration, his insides in knots. No two ways about it. Something was going to have to be done about this.

Rachel was not feeling casual as they returned to the car and started the long drive back to Iowa. She couldn't take her eyes off Craig as he concentrated on the highway, his strong hands steady and competent on the wheel. She noticed the way gold-tipped hair grew on the backs of his hands and how that same hair was thicker on his sinewy forearms, matching his tawny, intriguingly expressive eyebrows. She was aware of his clean scent and how he had tasted when he had kissed her, exciting and blatantly male. The memory of his mouth on hers still rocked her senses. Today, he had been anything but a man afraid to feel.

Then something occurred to her. She had freely shared her past with him this afternoon, but he had volunteered next to nothing about himself. What little he had told her had been unhappily, reluctantly revealed. So much about him was still private. It bothered her. His silence in the car bothered her, too. He seemed withdrawn suddenly, alone with his thoughts even when he turned his head to smile at her.

Rachel smiled back and wondered what was happening. Where was all this going, and where did she want it to go? She didn't know. In the end, it seemed wisest to wait and see.

He played the radio. An easy-listening station. The music relaxed her, and the smooth motion of the car was lulling. It had been a full day. She snuggled into a corner and fell asleep.

It was twilight when she wakened. The radio was silent, the car motionless. She stirred and sat up. They were back in Iowa. But not on the circus lot. The car was parked outside his motel. She turned on the seat to find Craig gazing at her with decisiveness on his face and a clear, urgent longing in his eyes.

Three

Her pulse accelerated at the look of need in his eyes. She knew what he wanted before he actually expressed it. There was something else she understood. This was no spontaneous urge spawned out of an impulsive male desire. He was ready to risk something vital here—only after a long, careful deliberation on the silent drive from Baraboo. She could hear what his decisiveness was costing him in his voice, deep and ragged with emotion.

"I don't want to play games, Rachel. I'm not going to pretend why I brought you here. You know why, and if you—"

He broke off, searching for the right words. She didn't try to help him. She waited, watching his face, admiring the sharply defined planes and angles in the shadowy light. It was a strong, masculine face, but at the moment, it was nervous. He was certain, but he was also scared. It was important to him that he not fail her or himself.

"Look," he said, struggling on, "I thought we were both feeling the same way and that if something was going to happen for us, you'd prefer it didn't happen at the circus lot where the others . . . Well, you know. But if I've made a big mistake and gone and assumed—" He hesitated again. "Anyway, if this is all wrong, if you don't want it to happen, then I'll take you straight back to the lot. Okay?"

This was ridiculous. She had a lump in her throat, and she wanted to cry. It was scarcely what the situation called for. She couldn't help it. He sounded uncharacteristically awkward and shy, so boyishly vulnerable that he made her remember what he had reluctantly revealed back at Baraboo. Growing up, he had never known the closeness of family. It was a need he had learned to deny in himself. But she was convinced that under the marine-style toughness was a solid, inherent decency longing for what it had missed. Yes, she wanted to cry.

"Rachel," he begged, "please, say something. You're sitting there just looking at me, and I'm going out of my mind."

She couldn't restore what he had lost as a child, but there was another essential closeness she could satisfy. She could give him what they both wanted and needed.

"You didn't make any mistake," she told him softly.

She could hear Craig expelling a long sigh of relief.

She unbuckled her seat belt, but before she reached for the door handle, she was impelled to add a quick, tremulous, "Craig, I—I'm not the most experienced woman in the world. It's not that I've never—well, you know. It's just that I felt you should understand."

"I don't want the most experienced woman in the world," he promised her. "Don't worry, we'll be good to each other."

He gave her all the confidence she needed. She smiled at him and slid from the car.

Seconds later, they were inside his room with the drapes drawn against the thickening twilight and he was groping for the switch on the bedside lamp. He turned to find her looking around the room, a small, knowing smile on her mouth.

"What?" he asked.

"It's so neat. Just like its occupant. No disorder, everything in place."

He grinned mysteriously. "You're wrong. This room is filled with clutter, just like every motel room I spent the night in since I joined Donelli's Circus."

"I don't see it."

He tapped his skull. "It's all in here. A whole lot of wild and wanton fantasies about the lady bareback rider. A real mess. It's been driving me crazy. I can't seem to clean it up. You'd be shocked at the jumble."

She moved across the room and stood in front of him by the bed. "Show me," she challenged him, her voice low and silky.

His eyes, hooded now, smiled at her seductively. "Suppose," he said, his voice husky with promise, "I sort them out for you. All the fantasies. One by one."

"Yes, suppose you do that."

"First," he instructed slowly, "I imagined myself looking at you. No interruptions, no objections. Just looking my fill."

"Yes," she said, encouragingly, as his gaze leisurely stroked her, exploring the contours of her face and body. His visual caresses were so prolonged, so intimate, that a sweet warmth began to steal through her vitals.

"And then?" she urged.

"And then," he said in a rich, resonant drawl, "I start to touch you. Like this."

His hand came to her face and began to drift over her features, lightly, lazily, his fingers stirring through the masses of her hair, then teasing the shell of one ear before coming to rest at her throat. He could feel her pulse dancing under his fingertips.

"After that," he whispered, "I hold you."

"How?" she demanded.

"This way." His arms went around her, drawing her snugly against his compact body until he could feel her softness from thighs to shoulders. His cheek rested against hers, permitting him to savor the smoothness of her olive skin, the subtle fragrance of her lustrous brown hair.

"I like your fantasies," she said, enjoying the possessiveness of his embrace, the strength of his cradling arms. "I like them a lot."

"Do you? Would you like to know more of them?"

"Yes, please."

"I warn you," he said, "they get pretty ferocious after this."

"How ferocious?"

"There's this." His mouth demonstrated, feathering kisses across her face.

"That's not so ferocious," she objected.

"No, not yet," he agreed. He drew back slightly, one thumb hooked under her chin to lift her face to the angle he desired. "But maybe this one..."

His parted mouth came down over hers in a full, deep joining. The fusion was so immediate, so intense, that she felt the room rocking under her. No gentle tremor this time, she realized. This was a real quake.

Her senses raced out of control as she answered his kiss, her tongue meeting the slick bolt of flesh boldly probing the recesses of her mouth. She pressed against him, filling herself with his male flavor, the clean, pure scent of him. It was a mutual striving; she could feel him straining to capture the essence of her.

The passion that flared between them was so primitive, so unexpectedly stunning, that they were both shaken by it when he finally released her.

"I think," he said, his voice slurred with desire, "that we've just passed the fantasy stage."

"Passed it?" She laughed breathlessly. "We *galloped* by it!"

"Yeah." She could see him swallow with eagerness. "Then in that case..."

The next few minutes were a blur. He must have drawn her down on the bed. They must have shed most of their clothing. Whether they undressed themselves with hasty, fumbling hands or whether they undressed each other, Rachel didn't know. None of it was clear to her. None of it registered. Not, anyway, until her vision was blasted by the sight of his raw male magnificence in a pair of cotton briefs as blue as his eyes and as tight as skin.

Suddenly, she didn't know where to look. Wherever her gaze shifted, he was powerfully, vitally there. A pair of brawny shoulders. A deep chest with a cloud of dark golden hair. Hard, hair-roughened thighs. Her hand on the quilted bedspread was so close to those thighs that she could feel their slow heat tempting her fingertips.

Light-headed, her breathing increasingly unsteady as she half reclined on the bed, she could see him being equally aware of her as he loomed above.

There was a constriction in Craig's throat, in his chest, as he stared at her. He had never seen a woman look more alluring or more delicately feminine in lacy bra and silken panties. Her skin was flushed, her green eyes wide and loving as they met his, her full bottom lip trembling with an invitation that was unintentionally sexy. And he had never wanted a woman more than he did her at this moment.

"Rachel," he crooned.

"What?" she whispered.

"Nothing. Just Rachel."

She was all he needed, and she was there for his taking. Yes. Now. His arms slid around her, gathering her against his chest, flesh to flesh, soft to hard. The sensation was incredible. For a moment, he just held her, relishing the heat and scent of her skin. And then he began to taste her, planting slow, moist kisses down the side of her throat, his descending mouth finding the valley between her breasts.

Rachel shuddered under his tender assault, her fingers tangled in the thick hair of his lowered head, wildly seeking stability. Her breasts, heavy and full now with desire, felt his grazing hands as he found the front clasp of her bra, parting the lacy garment. She welcomed his lips on her taut buds, arching against him as he drew a sensitive nipple deep into his mouth. His forceful tongue elicited small moans of pleasure from low in her throat.

It pleased Craig that he had the power to inflame her like this. His own arousal was equally potent, the tumescence in his briefs aching for fulfillment. He wanted all of her then, everything she had to offer. And everything that he could offer her—his hardness buried within her satin softness, their bodies locked in loving combat.

But when his hands dropped to the waistband of her panties, when his eager fingers slid beneath the silkiness in quest of her womanhood, memory surfaced through his raging senses.

Damn! He'd almost forgotten! Another minute and it would have been too late. He couldn't have stopped himself, and he would have hated himself afterward for not protecting her.

Rachel was puzzled when his hands stilled, then withdrew. She heard him groan with suppressed urgency as he shifted away from her. Her eyes flew open, turning to watch him groping in the drawer of the bedside table. There was a folder of materials on the table, and in his frustrated haste, he swept it to the floor.

"What is it? What's wrong? I thought we—"

"They're not in here," he growled. "I could have sworn—I must have left them in the bathroom along with the toothpaste."

"What?"

"Condoms," he muttered. "I bought them last night when I went out for toothpaste."

"Oh." She couldn't help her laughter then. "Pretty sure of yourself, weren't you?"

He grinned at her sheepishly. "Look, stay in the mood, will you? *Please* stay in the mood. I'll be right back."

Leaving her in this state was one of the most difficult things he'd ever done, but if he hurried... Leaping from the bed, he headed for the bathroom, offering Rachel an appealing view of a shapely male backside displayed to advantage in the snug briefs.

In the bathroom, Craig searched for the condoms and was frantic when he couldn't find them. They had to be here! But they weren't. Wait a minute. He'd been right the first time around. He *had* put them in the bedside drawer. They must have slid to the back when he'd jerked the drawer open, and in his anxiousness, he had overlooked them.

Flipping off the light, he tore back into the bedroom where Rachel was waiting for him. Her long, lush figure was no longer half reclining on the bed, elevated on one elbow in that inviting position that had churned his senses at the deepest level. Everything had changed in the brief moment he'd been out of the room. And everything was wrong.

She was perched now on the edge of the bed. She had slipped back into her shirt, which she'd retrieved from the floor, her tempting flesh primly covered again from hips to throat. There was something else she had rescued from the floor. The folder of materials he had carelessly left in the open and even more carelessly knocked from the table. The tight expression on her face as she gazed down at the yellow legal sheets gathered now on her lap wiped all thought of the misplaced condoms from Craig's mind.

Swearing savagely under his breath, he crossed the room in swift strides and tried to take the pencil-covered sheets from her. She held them away, out of his reach. When her eyes lifted and met his, there was such hurt and accusation in them that he wanted to take the damn things and rip them into shreds. Not that that would change anything. She had already glanced at the contents and drawn all the worst conclusions.

"Obviously," she told him coolly, "I wasn't meant to see any of this. I'm sorry if you think I was prying. I was only putting them back on the table, trying to preserve that tidiness you seem to need. I couldn't help seeing what's in here, not with 'Donelli's Circus' heading every page."

He stood over her,, feeling helpless and clumsy. "Rachel, I don't think you were prying. And I wasn't trying to hide anything from you. It's just that this wasn't exactly the moment for telling you about the list."

"When would have been the right moment, Craig?" she demanded. "After I'd slept with you maybe?"

He scowled at her. "What's that supposed to mean?"

"Nothing. I—I'm upset, that's all. But since I have seen what you've written here and since it does directly concern me, I believe I have the right to a few explanations."

He understood what she must be thinking about him, and he hated it. Wanting to change that, needing to comfort himself as well as her, maybe to ease the strained situation for both of them, he started to put his arms around her. But she leaned away from him, choking a little on her emphatic refusal. "No! Not that way! Not this time! And—and would you please not stand there like that, practically naked?" She reached down and snatched up his jeans from near her feet on the floor, thrusting them at him. "Here."

He dragged on the jeans, muttering another oath. Rachel eyed him. The jeans should have helped, but he didn't bother with a belt and they were slung too low on his lean hips for comfort. *Her* comfort. He remained shirtless, and his sleek, muscled chest was also disturbing. Even his big, bare feet were provocative to her. But she couldn't let the sight of him affect her. Not when she had this betrayal in her lap to deal with.

Quickly lowering her gaze, she tapped at the sheets she had scanned in his absence. "I knew you were preparing recommendations for the bank. All of us knew it and expected it. But I never dreamed the changes you'd be asking for would be these."

"Rachel," he pleaded with her, "I'm trying to save your circus."

"No, not this way. Not by cutting jobs and letting loyal employees go."

"It's reasonable," he argued. "Your payroll is too large. When a business is in trouble, the payroll is always the first thing to be examined and trimmed. It's like a lifeboat. No one can survive if the lifeboat is overloaded."

"That's callous! Cold-blooded and callous! To sacrifice—"

"All right," he said, cutting her off, "so maybe that's a bad analogy. But you still can't afford to be sentimental, not if you expect to save your show."

"I wouldn't want to save it if it meant hurting my family. Anyway, we've been doing all right. Our gates have been excellent."

"It's not enough, Rachel. Your expenses are still too great. This is the only practical solution."

"Is that how you see every business you troubleshoot, Craig? Nothing but the facts and figures? What about the people? Because a circus *is* people. *My* people."

He turned away to avoid her wounded gaze and began to pace restlessly around the room on his bare feet. Why did she make him feel so blasted guilty? He was only doing what his work called for—being sensible. "There are other circuses, other jobs, and if you provide them with strong references . . ."

She shook her head angrily. "No, I don't want to even consider it. Anyway, there isn't a single unnecessary job on Donelli's. Everyone on the show is needed."

"Then you didn't look very carefully at those recommendations."

"I saw enough." She glanced down, flipping rapidly through the pages. "Here, for instance. You want me to cut the band entirely from the show. What are we supposed to do about music without our windjammers? They're the pulse of every performance. They set the tempo for the acts, provide the cues."

"I realize that. I also know it's possible to use taped music. Other circuses do. I checked into it."

"*Canned* music on Donelli's!" She was horrified by the suggestion. "We're a traditional circus, and traditional circuses carry bands. You saw that today at Baraboo. I thought that was what the trip was all about, so you could better understand the circus."

He dragged an impatient hand through his rumpled hair, for once not caring that it wasn't neatly in place. "Rachel, Baraboo is a museum, a pleasant history of the past. You're supposed to be now and the future."

"I see. And you think I'm being unrealistic about that. I suppose you also think I'm not very responsible, that you couldn't trust me enough to consult with me about these proposed changes before you sent them off to the bank."

"What I think," he said with hands clenched at his sides, "is that you're not concerned enough with economy, and right now, that's the name of the game. And, no, I was not going to send my recommendations to the bank before I discussed them with you." He resented her implication that he wasn't being honest with her, that he might have sneaked the list off to the bank without her knowledge. "That's just a rough report there. I've been trying to tell you, when it was in final form, I planned to show it to you."

"Then since I have seen it," she insisted, "suppose we discuss it now."

He stopped pacing and leaned one hip against the long chest of drawers. He didn't want this. He didn't want any of it. But there was no avoiding it. "All right, we'll discuss it."

They went through each of his proposals. Craig recommended eliminating the cookhouse truck and tent. It was needless and costly. The performers and bosses had cooking facilities in their trailers, and the work crew could eat in town. Rachel said no. The company was a family, and families took their meals together.

Craig wanted to reduce the work crew. It was too large. She could save on salaries if she lightened the permanent force and hired part-time teenagers at lower wages on each of their stands. Rachel said no. All of the men were essential or they wouldn't be there.

Craig argued that the cat trainer should be replaced. His salary was astronomical and he was difficult to deal with, a womanizer who'd already caused conflict on the lot. Rachel said no. She agreed that Karl Dvorak could be temperamental, but he was their headliner. He drew the crowds. Besides, he had a season contract.

She could feel the frustration mounting for both of them as, one by one, Craig reviewed his recommendations and Rachel rejected them. Rachel knew he thought she was being impossible. She couldn't help it. All of his proposals involved terminating jobs, discharging the people she deeply cared for, and she couldn't bear to do that.

In the end, they were silent, at an impasse. She was miserable as she gazed at him across the room. He looked stiff and remote, not the warm and wonderful man she had shared Baraboo with, but a harsh stranger.

"What's going to happen?" she finally asked him softly, unhappily. "Is the bank going to force me to accept these changes if you submit them, whether I want them or not?"

He stood away from the chest of drawers, his voice flint hard. "No. That would constitute tortious interference. All the bank can do is advise and urge. Legally, you're still the owner and manager of Donelli's Circus. The final decisions are up to you."

His reassurance offered her only small relief. Maybe the bank couldn't insist she tighten her payroll by firing people, but she knew she risked their future support by a refusal to cooperate. And if she should fail to meet any interest payments on that debt . . . The prospect was frightening.

Leaving the folder on the bed, Rachel stood and began to pull on her slacks. She suddenly felt the need to return to the familiar security of the circus lot. She didn't want to stay here another moment. Being with Craig, feeling as they both did, simply hurt too much.

"What do you want me to do, Rachel?" he asked, grimness in his expression as he watched her search for her shoes.

"I want you to find other ways to save the show, something we can both live with."

"Like what?"

"I don't know. You're the expert. There must be alternatives." She found her shoes and slipped them on. "I'm going to call a taxi from the motel office."

"That's crazy. I'll drive you back to the lot."

She shook her head, reaching for her purse. "No, I—I'd rather call a taxi."

He didn't follow her to the door. He stood there, hands jammed into the pockets of his jeans. She couldn't get away from him fast enough, he realized. She thought he was an unfeeling bastard who wanted to put a lot of her people out of work. Damn it, he didn't enjoy cutting jobs, but sometimes, there was no other way. Only she was too stubborn to see the reality of the situation.

Rachel opened the door, then turned to consider him. "I thought after today," she said gently, "that I knew you, that under all that marine armor I was able to see a man with special sensitivities. Was I wrong, Craig?''

He stiffened. He didn't answer her. She waited a second, then murmured her thanks for Baraboo and slipped out of the room. He let her go.

When she was gone, he went on standing there. He'd made a big mistake today. He had opened a door, allowed himself to be vulnerable, and now he was paying the penalty. All the old pain was crowding inside, threatening to overwhelm him. Well, he could be determined, too. He would shut the door, lock it against the emotions he couldn't handle. He would go back to being an impersonal trouble-shooter on the circus lot, all business, nothing else. It was safer like that. Maybe the only way to survive.

Four

The circus moved on through the heartland, covering new
territory in Minnesota, then swinging south again. The
weather remained mild, and the attendance at each performance was encouraging.

Rachel didn't know whether Craig sent his recommendations to the bank or withheld them as she had urged. She
didn't ask. They were carefully avoiding each other as they
had before Baraboo. She guessed he hadn't submitted the
report or he wouldn't be there daily on the lot, still investi-
gating each department. He wasn't the kind of man to leave
a job unfinished, though she could see he was less than enthusiastic about his role. He was back to being a surly
stranger with the company, wearing his business suits again
like defiant barriers.

She overheard Felix tell Precious, "I knew that sweet
mood of his was too good to last."

Precious's laugh came out like a whistle through his missing teeth. "Yeah, makes you wonder what spoiled the guy's temper. For a while there, he was almost human."

The two men glanced at her, then exchanged meaningful looks. They knew darned well what was responsible for Craig's renewed gruffness. The whole company knew without being told. They also realized she was as unhappy as the troubleshooter. But Rachel didn't see what she could do about mending the situation, not when she and Craig had such opposing views on the subject of her circus. It made her wonder if they weren't hopelessly far apart on too many other levels to ever find the emotional intimacy she needed in a relationship. Just as well, then, that the clash occurred when it had, before they came impossibly involved. Still, she missed him deeply, and she felt guilty about the scene in his motel room.

It was her conscience, in fact, that prompted Rachel's impulsive gesture at the cookhouse party. They were back in Iowa, and Susi, the youngest member of the Rhee family, was observing her fifth birthday. The company never failed to celebrate holidays and birthdays together, particularly the children's. They were occasions for demonstrating that special closeness they all enjoyed.

Still in makeup and costume, they'd gathered around the long tables in the cookhouse tent between performances. It was a big, noisy event, all of them talking and laughing over each other, the youngest ones chasing each other happily between the tables. Dark-eyed Susi, flushed with excitement, perched on Rachel's lap as she opened her gifts. Her beaming parents were on either side while her brother, Kim, supplied unwanted instructions from across the table.

Rachel, along with the others, looked up with smiling expectancy as the oversize birthday cake was carried to the table by the cook and his helper. That was when she discovered Craig.

He stood at the edge of the tent, apart from the others. One arm looped around a pole, he negligently watched the festivities, his handsome face betraying no emotion. Rachel's senses quickened on her treacherously. Even like this, cold and remote, the sight of him provoked memories of the robust male body that had held her so forcefully, yet so tenderly, in his motel room.

Overcoming her weakness, she started to look away before their gazes met. But something prevented her from doing that. It was the look in his eyes. Even at this distance, with his expression carefully impassive, his whole attitude proclaiming a supreme indifference, she couldn't mistake the plain longing in his eyes. It was a hunger he wasn't even aware of conveying as he watched the proceedings.

Rachel remembered what her ringmaster had told her about Craig just before Baraboo. ... *The miserable kid who hasn't been invited to the party and swears he doesn't care when he really does care.* And she recalled what Craig, himself, had reluctantly revealed that afternoon by the river. He had grown up never knowing about family bonds, never experiencing the warmth and closeness of a secure family unit. Always on the outside looking in. He had denied his lonely state, told himself he had missed nothing. Just as he was doing now. But his eyes couldn't hide the truth.

Rachel ached for him. She couldn't stand this! Whatever his pride, she wanted him included. She wanted him inside, not outside. She wanted him to be a part of *this* family, at least for today.

The birthday cake with its five lighted candles was placed in front of a round-eyed Susi. With encouraging applause from all sides, she made her wish and blew out the candles. As Susi's mother started to cut the cake, Rachel had an inspiration. She leaned down and whispered secretively into Susi's ear, "How would you like to make someone very happy?"

An intrigued Susi whispered back, "Who?"

"See Mr. Hollister over there?"

"Yes."

"Why don't you take him the very first special slice of your cake?"

Susi hesitated, face scrunched up as she considered the suggestion.

Rachel nodded slowly. "I think it would really please him."

"Okay." She wriggled down from Rachel's lap, holding out her hands for the paper plate her mother passed to her.

The others watched in amused affection as the chubby five-year-old solemnly bore her offering along the aisle.

Craig was startled when Susi stopped in front of him and shyly, carefully extended the plate toward him. "Here. We want you to have the first piece. It's got one of the candles," she explained.

Rachel watched Craig's face, fascinated by the deep blush of embarrassed pleasure that spread from his collar to his ears. That he was capable of such a reaction touched her. He reached for the plate, accepting it with an awkward, hoarse, "Thank you, Susi."

Delighted by his response, Susi's mouth split into a wide grin, her small body squirming in pleasure. Then something went wrong. Craig stiffened, his expression suddenly twisting as he stared down at her.

With the others looking on, muttering their indignation now, he shoved the untouched cake on the corner of the nearest table, turned around and strode wordlessly away from the tent.

Rachel jumped up from her place and hurried to Susi. Her bottom lip was wobbling unhappily. "He didn't want it, Rachel. He left it."

"It's all right, sweetheart. Maybe he's just not hungry right now."

Buster joined them. "Come on, Susi, we've got lots more cake to cut and pass around."

Buster, almost as small as Susi, took her back to the head table, leaving Rachel to stare after Craig's retreating figure. Damn him. There was no excuse for his rudeness, for treating Susi like that. She wasn't going to let him get away with it, either. Not this time!

Rachel caught up with Craig where he had stopped at the back side of the big top. Arms over his head, he was clutching one of the taut stake lines, as though he needed something to hang on to.

"It's one thing to offend the adults in the company," she angrily addressed his rigid back, "but did you have to go and hurt a five-year-old like that?"

Head lowered, refusing to turn around, he muttered something she failed to understand. She hoped it was an apology, but she couldn't be sure.

"I don't understand you," she persisted. "Why do you deliberately alienate my family every time one of them tries to be kind to you?"

He was still unwilling to face her, but this time, he lifted his head and she was able to clearly hear his brittle words. "*Family*. You keep calling them *family*. They're not your family, Rachel. They're employees."

"You just can't accept that sort of kinship we share, can you?" she challenged him. "Why, Craig? *Why?*"

His hands dropped from the stake line. He turned reluctantly to confront her. His face was so hollow eyed with pain that Rachel was instantly contrite. This wasn't what she had expected. "Craig? What is it? What's wrong?"

How could he tell her? How could he begin to explain that the mere body language of a child had triggered a wrenching memory of another five-year-old who had grinned and wriggled for him in the exact same expression of secret pleasure? A cruel reminder he hadn't been able to handle. It would sound so weak and stupid trying to make her understand. Besides, he didn't want to talk about it. He was too chewed up inside to discuss it with anyone.

"What do you want from me, Rachel?" he asked her tiredly.

"I just want you to give them a chance, that's all. Let them see the man I saw at Baraboo. They're good people, Craig. They want to accept you if you'd give them a reason to."

"I don't need that kind of acceptance," he informed her coldly.

"Not to belong? I don't believe that."

He stared at her for a second, then shook his head, his voice curt. "Just let me alone to do the job the bank is paying me to do. *All* of you."

He turned abruptly and walked away, heading for his car.

Fine, she thought, glaring after the lone figure. From now on, she would do exactly that, because he didn't want or deserve anything better than his bitter solitude.

But when he disappeared around the curve of the big top, her resentment subsided and she drooped against the stake line. What was she going to do about him? He had gotten to her, emotionally and physically. She couldn't pretend she hadn't and simply ignore his existence, no matter what he insisted.

Rachel was roused from her listlessness when she felt a pair of eyes trained on her. She looked up, identifying the source of the inquisitive gaze. Napoleon's cage was parked close by. The chimp was pressed against the bars, his wise old face watching her sympathetically, as though he had heard and understood the whole scene.

She crossed to the cage, unlatched the door and swung it open. In other days, Napoleon would have celebrated his release by bounding into her arms and hooting joyfully. But he was no longer so active, his health having deteriorated with advanced age. Now he preferred the security of his cage, rarely emerging, though he welcomed her company. Rolling his mobile lips in greeting, he gently touched her face when she crouched by the open door.

The chimp's keeper kept a supply of sunflower seeds on top of the cage to tempt his charge. They were Napoleon's favorite treat. Rachel reached for the seeds, extending a handful to coax the animal to eat. She was concerned by his declining appetite and steady weight loss, but there was little to be done. Napoleon hesitated and then politely, daintily picked the seeds from her hand, one by one. Even in his stronger days, he had always been well-mannered, disdaining any greed.

He slowly munched on the seeds, keeping his sad eyes on Rachel's face as she talked to him softly. As a child growing up on the circus, Napoleon had been her special confidant. When no human would do, she had confessed her heartaches and girlhood secrets to the chimpanzee. He had listened, and she had felt consoled. That hadn't changed.

"Am I wrong, Napoleon? Am I being too stubborn about everything? What do you think? Maybe it is me. Maybe I'm not trying hard enough to understand him. But he is impossible. All that tough pride. Okay, okay, so he excites me. But that's not enough, is it?

"One day he's going to be gone, Napoleon. He's going to finish what he's trying to do here, and then he'll pick up and just disappear. I probably won't see him again. That scares me. I don't want it to scare me. I don't want to care like that.

"You know it could never work for us, Napoleon. Because we're too different. Because there are too many problems and no solutions. He realizes that. That's why he's keeping out of my way. I know it, too. So, then, why can't I stop caring?"

Napoleon ate his seeds and grunted while he soothingly stroked her arm. The magic bond between animal and woman was still there. Rachel felt less troubled when she returned to the cookhouse tent.

Several days later, the show was on a rare three-day stand in southern Michigan when Felipe Ortega came to her. The amiable, Mexican-born aerialist and his brothers, Julio and Tito, were featured fliers on Donelli's Circus. It was just after the evening performance, and Felipe was still wearing his richly decorated cape over his spangled tights when he drew her aside in the backyard.

"Rachel, can you be in the stands first thing tomorrow morning when we practice?"

She caught the excitement in his low voice. "Of course, Felipe. Why? What's up?"

"I need a witness there. Someone official, you know. We feel like tomorrow's the day for sure. I'm ready for it, Rachel. I'm gonna catch the quad!"

No one knew better than Rachel how important Felipe's dream was to him. He longed to master the rare and difficult quadruple somersault. Actually, in practice sessions, the young trapezist had already repeatedly thrown the quad. But he had yet to link up with his brother, Tito. If he could successfully manage it, the feat would be added to the regular act and he would join the roster of trapeze greats.

"Felipe, that's wonderful! You certainly deserve it. You've worked hard enough for it. I'll be there, and I won't say a word to anyone."

Rachel should have known that her promised silence counted for nothing. As always, the news managed to spread, and the next morning, the whole company crowded into the big-top stands, tense and expectant, praying for Felipe's victory.

Molly sat beside Rachel as they watched a pair of riggers raise the safety net into position under the trapeze apparatus above the ring.

Rachel knew how risky the stunt was. "I don't suppose there's any chance I could convince Felipe to wear a mechanic," she said to Molly, referring to the safety harness and controlled line used in practice sessions.

Molly shook her head. "It wouldn't count then. Don't worry. He'll be okay. Julio says Felipe is really up for it today."

The three brothers appeared in their practice leotards. Felipe, wrapping protective linen around his wrists, searched for Rachel in the stands. He caught her eye, and she signaled a thumbs-up sign. The teenager grinned back, teeth snow white in his dusky face. Devout Catholics, the brothers crossed themselves and began to climb the narrow ladders toward their lofty perches.

It was a warm morning. The canvas side walls had been lowered to encourage the circulation of air, but it was still hot and humid under the big top. Molly had found a discarded program from last evening's performance and was using it to fan herself slowly. She stopped suddenly, nudging Rachel with the program to draw her attention to the performers' entrance aisle just beside where they sat.

Rachel didn't need the warning. She had already sensed Craig's nearness. It was frightening how she never failed to be conscious of his presence. Worse, he was so close this morning that she could actually feel his body heat, though she tried to ignore what that did to her.

Offering a stony profile, he didn't speak to her or glance their way as he stood in the aisle. He was still alone, withdrawn. She knew he didn't want to be here, to be among them again and yet not a part of them. But it seemed to be something he couldn't help in himself. She wished she understood that.

Craig was watching what was happening above the ring. Rachel made a concentrated effort to do the same.

Felipe had reached the platform, his brother behind him. Julio would remain there to coach Felipe and manage his trapeze for him. The muscular Tito, facing them from his end of the rigging, launched himself and began to swing rhythmically out over the ring, his powerful legs wrapping securely around the ropes as he dropped down from his bar.

Felipe, poised on the pedestal board above the platform, gripped his bar and fastened his gaze on his catcher. The timing had to be split-second perfect. His lithe, athletic figure, religiously conditioned with daily training, tensed with readiness. The suspended Tito smacked his hands together, more in encouragement than as a signal. It was Julio who called the sharp command, "Go!"

Felipe lobbed himself into space on his trapeze and began to pump for the precious required height, his body reaching for the canvas. Rachel had watched the young man work like this scores of times, but the style and fluid form of the flier, the seeming ease masking an enormous effort, always had her holding her breath. The whole gathering, faces upturned, was hushed, hopeful.

At the precise instant of readiness, Felipe left his bar and went soaring into a high arc, his body in an imperative tight tuck as it hurtled into the revolutions. One. Two. Three. Four. Then Julio shouting, "Break!"

Felipe, all awareness sacrificed to the dizzy spins, depended at this stage on his two brothers. His body obeyed, straightening, extending, straining for the connection with Tito. It didn't happen. Once again, the quad had been thrown but not successfully caught. There were groans of shared disappointment from the stands.

The flier plummeted toward the safety net, twisting in midair in order to cushion himself against the impact with back and buttocks. To land any other way could cost an aerialist a broken neck. Discouragement was not in Felipe's vocabulary. Bouncing to the edge of the net, he gripped, flipped himself over gracefully between the spreader ropes and headed again for the ladder.

Rachel began to lose count of his repeated efforts to link up with the hanging Tito. Again, and then still again, came the takeoffs from the pedestal board, the flipping body hugged into a close ball to reduce wind resistance, the stretching out, the disappointing dives into the safety net.

Rachel by then was sweating for her friend. She knew it was a brutal, punishing business and also a dangerous one. At that speed, better than eighty miles an hour, there was the risk of the flier crashing into his catcher or a wrong landing in the net thirty-seven feet below.

But with each descent came Felipe's fiercely promised, "I won't leave it down in the net! Not today!"

"This is no good," Molly said worriedly. "He's exhausting himself."

Rachel shook her head. "His body won't know it's tired until he quits. He'll do it."

And he did minutes later! Once more came the high lift, the fast four turns, the clean break. This time looked no different to Rachel than the others, but some small rightness must have been there, because suddenly there came the solid whack of four hands gripping four wrists.

For a stunned instant, there was silence as the two joined brothers swung back and forth over the ring. Felipe and Tito weren't sure it had happened until Julio began to yell with excitement while the stands below burst into wild cheers.

Molly grabbed Rachel and hugged her joyfully. "I'm so proud of him I could cry!"

Rachel laughed and hugged her back. She was turning from Molly's embrace when her glance fell on Craig. Unable to resist the moment, he was grinning happily. It pleased her that he could forget himself long enough to share in Felipe's triumph.

He felt her gaze and turned his head, his expression suddenly sober as their eyes met. They exchanged a long, intimate look that left Rachel breathless. And then she felt Molly's hand on her arm, urging her to join the rest of the company as it poured from the stands. The brothers had descended from their perches and well-wishers were surrounding them with noisy congratulations.

Rachel got to her feet, intending to follow. But she stopped where she was. Through the open sides of the big top, her attention was caught by the sight of a familiar figure strolling across the lot toward the tent. Her heart slid in the direction of her stomach. She could think of only one reason why Hank Sutherland, the president of the bank holding the mortgage on Donelli's Circus, would travel all this distance from St. Louis. Craig must have sent those recommendations for job cuts to the bank, after all, and Sutherland was here to see whether the changes had been implemented. She hated to think Craig would have done this against her wishes, but what other explanation could there be?

Her gaze went sharply to Craig, who was still standing in the aisle beside her. She saw that he, too, was aware of the banker's arrival. What's more, he had sensed her panic and the reason for it.

He looked at her, his face blank but his voice rough with irritation. "Don't worry. It isn't what you think. He's not here to check on you. He's here to check on *me*."

Without further explanation, Craig abruptly left her side and strode off across the arena to meet the banker. Rachel stared after him, perplexed. Here was something else to baffle her, like the mystery of his behavior when Susi had offered him the cake.

Rachel went down into the ring to pay her tribute to the elated Ortegas, but all the while, she kept an eye on the figures of the two men who were standing just outside the big top. She couldn't hear their exchange, but she could see that Craig wasn't pleased. He looked tense and annoyed. In the end, the banker placed a reassuring hand on his shoulder. Craig nodded reluctantly, then turned and walked away, leaving Hank Sutherland gazing after him with a pensive, anxious expression on his face.

Rachel broke away from the mob in the ring and went to join the banker. He was a spare man with salt-and-pepper hair and a reddish moustache. He seemed happy to see her and shook her hand warmly.

"It looks like I came in on some excitement," he said, his gray eyes smiling at her.

Rachel explained about the stunt Felipe had executed before venturing a curious, "You know you're always welcome, Mr. Sutherland, but it is a surprise seeing you all this way from St. Louis."

"Oh, there's a reason. My wife and I are visiting my daughter and her family. They live right over here in Lansing. In fact, I'm planning on bringing the grandchildren to your performance this afternoon, but knowing how tied up you'll be at showtime, I thought I'd just run by this morning to say hello."

Rachel assumed this was his opening for asking her about the circus's current financial situation. To her surprise, that concern was not mentioned. There was something else on his mind.

"So, tell me, Rachel, how are you and your people getting along with Craig Hollister?"

It was a question she wasn't prepared for. "He's—well, sometimes a little difficult to work with. Though always conscientious," she added quickly, wanting to be honest, but disliking the thought of betraying Craig.

The banker nodded soberly. "Yes, the way he resisted the assignment from the start, I was afraid of that. He wasn't in a very good mood with me just now. He resents my coming here, of course. He thinks I'm fussing. Not about his work with you," he assured her obscurely, then broke off to gaze thoughtfully again in the direction Craig had gone.

"The thing is," he went on after a moment, "I had hoped his being here in this kind of setting would make a difference, that it would be just the change he needs, but so far..." He shook his head. "Well, maybe yet."

"I—I don't understand."

"I know I'm being vague about this. I guess what I'm asking, Rachel, is for you to be patient with him. There's a good reason for our proud ex-marine's hard moods."

She waited for the banker's explanation, but he must have felt he had made his point without having to confide what Craig would probably regard as no one else's business. In any case, he changed the subject entirely with a cheerful, "Now, if you'll just tell me where I can get one of those teddy-bear clowns, I'll get out of your hair and let you get back to running your circus."

Rachel was bewildered by his request. "Teddy-bear clowns? I don't—"

"Like that one." He pointed behind her. "It would make a big hit with my granddaughter."

She turned in the direction he indicated. Susi Rhee was sitting cross-legged on the grass deep under the nearest big-top bleacher section. It was a favorite retreat for the little girl, just as it had been for Rachel as a child when she had sought one of those private, nonadult worlds in which to spin her dreams. Susi was talking softly to the companion on her lap—a teddy bear dressed as a circus clown. Rachel had never seen it before, or one like it.

"Excuse me, Mr. Sutherland, while I play detective for you."

Stepping through the stake line, she ducked under the stand and knelt beside Susi in the grass. "Hi, sweetie. Can I ask you something?"

Susi, concentrating on arranging the clown's ruff around the bear's neck, nodded without looking up. "Uh-huh."

"Where did you get your new bear? I don't remember seeing him before."

"He was a birthday present."

"He's very handsome and just perfect for the circus. But, honey, I was at your party when you opened all your presents, and he wasn't one of them."

"Yes, he was. Only not at the party. That man gave him to me afterwards. I think it was the next day."

"What man, Susi?"

"I forget his name. The one who didn't want his cake."

Rachel stared in surprise at the bear. "Mr. Hollister, you mean?"

"Uh-huh. He said he didn't know it was my birthday before the party, so he had to buy my present for me after that." She held up the bear for Rachel's approval. "He's called Toots."

"That's a good name for a teddy-bear clown," Rachel said slowly, awed by the knowledge that under that implacable hide Craig wore like plates of cold steel lurked a softy. Whatever his tough attitude that day, he must have ultimately cared enough about hurting Susi to go out of his way to show her how sorry he was. So, in spite of his denials, people did matter to him. Children, anyway. It was a satisfying affirmation of what she'd already suspected.

"Thank you, Susi." Rachel crawled out of the cool shade under the stands and stood, dusting her hands as she faced the waiting banker. "Sorry, Mr. Sutherland, I don't know where the bear came from." Something told Rachel that Craig wouldn't appreciate having either her or the banker know what he had done.

"That's too bad. I thought maybe the circus sold the bears on one of its souvenir stands."

"Afraid not, though it isn't a bad idea. I'll have to look into it."

"Yes, I think they'd be very popular."

The banker parted from her a moment later, leaving Rachel more frustrated than ever by the intriguing enigma of Craig Hollister. And in the bargain, even more hopelessly, unwisely attracted to him.

It was well after midnight when Craig returned to the circus lot. His old insomnia—one of the worst symptoms of the long torment he had suffered but which he thought he had overcome weeks ago—had reoccurred this evening. Not only had he not been able to sleep, his motel room had felt like a jail cell. His body, as restless as his troubled mind, had craved air and activity. For once careless about his dress, he had thrown on a pair of jeans and an old crewneck sweater and escaped the motel.

Now, sitting in his car parked on the side of the lot, he wondered why he had permitted himself to be lured back to the circus. If it were just air and exercise he needed, he could have walked the streets in town or found a deserted park somewhere. Why did he end up here, when this place and its people represented the conflict he had to contend with daily? Why did he punish himself? He didn't want to wrestle with the answer to that question. He was afraid of it.

Dragging a hand impatiently through his blond hair, Craig pocketed his keys and left the car. The heat of the day was only a memory. There was a rawness in the air now, and a mist was rising from the long grass of a nearby meadow. He shivered a little, glad of the sweater he was wearing.

He began to stroll aimlessly around the grounds. Except for a few security lights, the lot was dark. There was no one around to challenge him, though he did glimpse through the open door of one of the trailers a night watchman taking a coffee break. Nothing stirred except the softly rattling chains of the elephants at their hobbles. He had never seen the circus when it wasn't as active as a rush hour. To find it completely at rest like this was an appealing, strangely magical experience.

Craig paused outside one of the trailers. It was as shadowy and silent as the others. Its occupant must be asleep. He knew the trailer was Rachel's. For a long time, he gazed at the closed door, as afraid of his longing as the answers he'd resisted a moment ago in the car.

Regretting his weakness, he turned away and began to wander once more across the lot. He realized it was also regret that had kept him awake in the motel, mostly because of his attitude with Hank this morning. He was sorry about that. The banker was only trying to be a friend.

Craig knew he was living with a lot of regrets these days. Too many of them. He wasn't sure what he could do about it. Sometimes, he felt so damn defenseless over the subject that he wanted to smash things in his frustration. It was that way with Rachel and her people. He wished he could be comfortable with them, worthy of their casual friendships, if not their closeness. But he didn't know how to join them, how to begin. He had lost that ability, or maybe he had never possessed it.

Anyway, what was the point in trying to build relationships that could go nowhere? Just as soon as he found the elusive key to rescuing the circus, he would be leaving here. So why get involved and then have to endure the even more painful regret of separation? Yeah, he knew about the misery of separation, all right.

Hank Sutherland had urged him not to rush it. The banker would be happy if he lingered here all summer. Maybe he expected a miracle. But Craig didn't think there could be any miracles for him. Besides, there was another reason why he needed to finish here and get away. He no longer trusted himself where Rachel was concerned.

Avoiding the stake line, which could be risky in the dark, he slowly worked his way around the curve of the big top. It was when he neared the front side of the great tent that he noticed through the canvas the softly suffused glow of a burning work lamp. It surprised him. He wondered who was inside this late and what they were doing.

He headed toward the big top's front door, the light tempting him like a warm beacon.

Five

"**W**hat is it?" Craig demanded. "What's wrong?"

Startled by his deep voice over her head, Rachel looked up in surprise from the thick blanket spread on the ground. She was huddled there, her arms locked around legs drawn against her breasts. She must have dozed off for a second with her face pressed to her knees. She hadn't been aware of Craig's arrival.

Craig watched her lift her head slowly from her knees, one slim hand brushing back from her face the curtain of warm brown hair enriched by the glow of the solitary work lamp behind her. Her face was flushed and sleepy as she gazed at him from under the sweep of those incredibly long eyelashes. Like him, she was wearing jeans and a sweater against the chill of the evening. The sweater hugged the swell of her breasts provocatively. He had never seen her look so desirable.

Rachel, staring up at him, was conscious of his sexuality. Craig's face, looming over her, had the look of a fallen angel's. There was a golden stubble of beard on his jawline from the late hour, the care lines around his eyes and mouth more pronounced in the shadowy light, his hair attractively tousled. To see him like this, for the first time not perfectly groomed, was a rather awesome revelation. And a pleasure.

It was Craig who broke the spell between them. He looked off into the still gloom, realizing that she was alone in the vastness of the big top. He also noticed that the chimpanzee's cage was parked close to the blanket. He faced her again, one of his quirky, tawny eyebrows lifting in puzzlement.

"What's going on?" he asked, concern in his rough voice.

Before she could answer him, there was the sound of a low, raspy cough from inside the open cage. Instantly alert, Rachel scooted forward on her knees. Head and hands inside the cage, she spent a moment fussing and making soothing, murmuring sounds.

Craig hunkered down on the blanket beside her, trying to understand. "What are you doing?"

"He's restless and frightened," she told him. "He senses what's happening. I'll have to hold him."

"Can I help?" *What is happening?* he wondered.

"It's okay. He doesn't weigh that much. He never did, but these days..." She broke off to concentrate on gathering the chimp carefully into her arms. He was clinging to her like a baby, arms curled around her neck, as she withdrew from the cage, settling herself down on the blanket.

Napoleon didn't seem to mind Craig's presence. Rachel, too, accepted his company. She didn't think to question why he was here late at night on the lot, looking as he did. It just seemed natural and right that he had joined her in what she expected to be a long, unhappy vigil.

Craig watched her as she shifted the animal into a more comfortable position in her arms. He noticed that the chimp's breathing was slow and labored. "He's sick," he said. "How bad is it?"

Rachel shook her head, her voice surprisingly calm. "He's dying."

Craig stared at her, a little shocked over her control. "What's wrong with him?"

Cradling the chimp, she rocked him gently. He quieted in her arms, the sad old eyes searching her face trustingly. "Technically," she explained over Napoleon's head, "it's a congestive heart condition, and there's nothing to be done about it. It comes with old age, for animals as well as people. And Napoleon, in chimp years, is very old. Almost fifty."

"I didn't know," Craig muttered.

"Well, none of us talked about it much, but we've been expecting this for some time. He's failed a lot in the last few days. I don't think he'll last the night."

"And you're camping out in here to be with him while he—" Craig couldn't bring himself to say it.

"Of course. I wouldn't be anywhere else. I could never let him die alone."

Craig nodded, then scowled. "The others shouldn't have left you all on your own to face this."

"Wayne, his keeper, would have stayed. Felix, too. But there's nothing they can do. I sent them away after we dragged the cage in here. I wanted Napoleon out of the night air and away from the other animals. Besides, I need Felix and Wayne to stick close to one of our mares who's about to foal." She smiled poignantly at Craig. "Ironic, isn't it? One life about to go, another about to be born."

"Rachel—"

"No, it's all right. I'm a vet, remember? I can handle it."

He wasn't so sure about that. He now knew what the chimp meant to her. In any case, he had made up his mind to spend the night here with her. He wasn't going to let her deal with this alone, despite her courage and confidence.

And she'd better not object to that. She didn't say a word as he arranged himself on the blanket beside her. In fact, she seemed to welcome him. They sat in companionable silence while Napoleon drowsed in her arms, snoring softly.

"Rachel," Craig said after a moment, "if it's hopeless for him, wouldn't it be best to—you know, put him to sleep?"

She shook her head slowly but firmly. "If he were in pain, I wouldn't hesitate to do that. He's not. It's just uncomfortable for him, though I have softened that with a sedative. Napoleon is family, in his own way, and I want him to go with love and dignity, not the jab of a needle."

Craig nodded, respecting her sentiment. They were silent again, and then the chimp began to stir once more. Rachel tried to put him down in her lap to relieve her aching arms, but Napoleon refused the position. He wanted to be held against her breasts, like a scared infant.

"Here," Craig suggested, "let me try holding him for a turn. You can't support him like that all night."

She hesitated. "I'm not sure he'll let you, but all right."

She passed the chimpanzee to Craig, who gathered him carefully against his chest. Napoleon squirmed, looking for a moment as though he wouldn't accept the change. But then he nestled against Craig with a soft grunt, his fingers weakly plucking at the hairs on the back of one of Craig's hands.

"What's he doing?"

"He's trying to groom you," Rachel explained. "It's a sign of trust and affection."

"Oh." Craig looked pleased.

Napoleon's effort lasted only a few seconds. Then his arm dropped. He blinked, coughed once and went still again. A single moth fluttered around the work lamp on its metal standard. Rachel watched it, and then she began to talk about the chimpanzee in a low, loving voice.

"I can't imagine what Donelli's will be like without Napoleon. He's always been here, a part of the circus. More than my lifetime, anyway. I was told my grandmother bottle raised him when his mother rejected him. Maybe because he was a runt. He stayed small, but he never stopped being sweet tempered. That's unusual, because most chimps get aggressive after seven or eight years old, especially males. Not Napoleon. He responded to kindness. Sometimes, he seemed more human to me than some people I've known.

"We could have left him behind in winter quarters this season when it was obvious he was fading. He would have been well cared for there. I wouldn't do that. I wanted him where he'd always belonged right to the end, even if he could no longer perform or be displayed. He was something in his day. He did it all. Walked the tightrope, rode a horse, worked with the clowns. Cleverest animal I've ever known...."

Craig, gently swaying the chimpanzee, listened to her without comment. She seemed to need the comfort of reminiscing about Napoleon, and he didn't mind. It promised to be a long night, and he intended to be here for her through it all.

He should have known, however, that her supportive circus family would never have left her entirely alone to face this ordeal, whatever her instructions to them. Through the slow hours, one by one, they slipped into the tent to check on her and to hear the latest on Napoleon's condition. Most of them were in their nightclothes and looking sleepy, having roused themselves from their beds.

They were surprised to find Craig there with her. Some of them, the more protective ones, gazed at him suspiciously, but no one remarked on his presence. Instead, they offered to bring them coffee. Rachel said no. She had brought a thermos with her, and there was an extra cup for Craig if he wanted it. They nodded an acceptance to that, murmured their concern, and then wandered out again.

Mostly, though, Rachel and Craig were on their own in the quiet corner of the big top, taking turns holding Napoleon. It was an oddly intimate situation they shared, one that invited confidences of an emotional nature that in other circumstances would be resisted. But why not? Craig thought. It happened like this for people who kept watch together at the bedside of a dying friend or relative. And this experience was exactly like that. Maybe that's why he was able to open up and talk to Rachel as he finally did, tell her some things he hadn't been able to divulge that day at Baraboo.

"Like Napoleon here," he said in a low, even voice, "I was a runt, too, as a baby. Undernourished and ailing, they tell me. I don't know, maybe that's why my mother, whoever she was, abandoned me. Maybe she wasn't able to care for me. I'd like to think she had a good reason for leaving me like that, that she didn't just walk away with complete indifference."

Rachel, watching his impassive face, asked softly, "Did you ever try to trace her, find out who she was?"

His broad shoulders lifted in a small shrug. "I used to think about it once. I guess any kid would. But there was never anything to go on, not a clue." He paused thoughtfully, then went on. "The state family services couldn't offer me for adoption when I was in that condition. I must have been four or five before I was really strong and well."

"That's not beyond the age for couples wanting to adopt," she pointed out.

"No," he said slowly and with a slight reluctance now. "No, it isn't. I—I was adopted, Rachel." He shook his head. "It was never finalized."

"What happened, Craig?" she asked him gently.

He smiled wryly. "It all went wrong. Their marriage was in trouble before they ever got me. They had the old, stupid idea that a kid could make it solid again. Of course, they managed to keep that from family services. Well, it didn't work. I wasn't the answer. They split up before the adoption was made fully legal, and I went back to a foster home. After that . . . well, I didn't want any part of another adoption, even if someone had been interested. I thought I was to blame for that couple breaking up, that I'd failed somehow to be what I was supposed to be, even though a counselor tried to convince me it was never my fault."

Rachel offered no word of sympathy, knowing Craig's pride wouldn't appreciate it. Not at this point, anyway. But she silently damned the selfish couple who, in using him like that, had been as responsible as his birth mother for instilling in him a sense of unworthiness that must have haunted him all his life.

"Craig, wasn't there any foster home where you felt close, a real part of the family?"

"Should have been, shouldn't there? I guess they tried, some of them. Maybe it was me. Maybe I was too scared to trust any of them. I knew those foster homes weren't permanent. So why get close, why count on anything one week when the next week, for one reason or another, the family could no longer keep you?"

"But you could count on the marines," she remembered.

"Yeah, I could count on the marines."

"Only you left the corps," she pointed out. "You didn't make it your whole life."

"That's right, I left the corps when I was twenty-nine."

And he was what now? In his midthirties at least. What had he been doing with his life since the marines, other than building a career as a financial troubleshooter? She would have asked him, but he suddenly, emphatically changed the subject.

"I think I'd like some of that coffee now." He reached for the thermos on the blanket. "How about you?"

"No, thanks." She bent her head to check on Napoleon. He was asleep again in her arms, resting quietly for the moment.

She glanced back at Craig. His expression had tightened. He had shut down on her again, retreating behind his old armor. He had talked freely about his childhood, but he was clearly not ready to share anything personal about those years after the marines. There must be a strong reason for that. Hank Sutherland had suggested as much to her. Something traumatic, something Craig couldn't bear to discuss. But when he was able to talk about it—and she prayed he would trust and confide in her—she promised herself that she would be there to listen, offering whatever understanding and support he needed.

Through the night, they continued to warm and comfort the frail chimpanzee, sheltering him in their arms. Sometimes, overcome with fatigue, they napped between relieving each other. Rachel curled up on the blanket as she dozed. Craig preferred stretching out full length on the bottom tier of the lowest bleacher.

She watched him as he slept, wondering how he could endure the narrow hardness of the long planks. But mostly, she just admired his lean male form, one knee drawn up, an arm flung out over his head. His T-shirt had worked out of the waistband of his jeans along one side, riding up with his sweater to bare a teasing glimpse of the firm, hair-roughened flesh of his stomach. The sight made her a little woozy.

Felix found them like this when he marched into the tent. He glowered down at Craig. "What's *he* doing here?"

"Never mind," she whispered severely. "Did you need me?"

Felix tugged at his ancient fedora and grunted. "Yeah, it's the mare."

"Is she going into labor?"

"Looks like it."

"Trouble?"

"Don't think so, but I figured you ought to have a look. Just to make sure. How's Napoleon?"

"Not good, but he's hanging on." Bearing the weight of the drooping chimp, Rachel struggled to her feet and moved to the bleacher, gazing down at Craig's sleeping figure. She hated to rouse him. He looked so peaceful like this, the hard lines and taut guardedness smoothed away from his handsome, virile face.

"Craig," she called to him reluctantly.

He stirred and sat up, immediately alert. "Yeah, I'm here."

"I need to go and check on the mare. Can you take over for a bit?"

"Give him to me."

Rachel transferred the chimp to his waiting arms and then departed with Felix.

A half hour later, slipping back alone into the tent, she was startled by the scene of man and animal in the pool of lamp light. Craig was down on the blanket, tenderly rocking Napoleon in his arms, singing to him slowly, softly in his rich baritone.

"'Hush, little baby, don't say a word, Papa's gonna buy you a mockingbird. And if that mockingbird don't sing, Papa's gonna buy you a diamond ring....'"

Holding back in the still shadows, Rachel caught her breath, deeply moved by the sight and sound of what she was witnessing. Where had he learned that old lullaby that seemed so familiar to him? To whom had he sung it? She knew she could never bring herself to ask.

She didn't want to interrupt. She wanted to go on listening to the calming, sweet crooning of his voice. It was Craig who ended the magic. He must have finally sensed her standing there. Abruptly breaking off, he looked up. There was an endearing stain of embarrassment on his face that had her swallowing past the sudden tightness in her throat.

"He started to fuss," Craig explained with a sheepish, lopsided smile, "so I— Anyway, he's quiet now."

Rachel moved forward into the light, her vet's bag at her side. "I'd better check him over again," she said casually. She wisely didn't comment on the lullaby. Craig looked grateful.

"How's the mare?"

"Fine, but it will be a while yet before she delivers. Felix and Wayne between them can handle it. No sign of complications."

She joined him on the blanket.

It was close to daybreak when Napoleon lost the long fight and began to slip away. Rachel found it heartbreaking to listen to his feeble struggles to breathe, watching his increasing inertia, and knowing her medicine was powerless to help him. Toward the end, she did tranquilize him again, and that seemed to ease him through the worst.

She insisted on being the one to hold him when the time came. It was nothing dramatic or wrenching for the chimpanzee. He simply stopped breathing and sagged in her arms, like a child gone to sleep.

Rachel checked his vital signs, then met Craig's woeful gaze with a simple, whispered, "He's gone."

It was Craig who took over then, handling what was necessary at this moment because he feared Rachel was incapable of acting. He removed the limp Napoleon from her arms, laid him gently in his cage and covered him with the spare blanket he had used to pillow his head on the bleacher. Then he went back to Rachel, squatting in front of her and taking her hands consolingly in his.

"Are you going to be okay?" he asked worriedly.

The deep, comforting concern in his blue eyes penetrated her numbness. "Yes, I'm all right." She smiled at him thinly.

He expected tears. But she didn't cry. She seemed to have her grief firmly under control now. He wasn't sure if that was a good sign or a bad one, but he wasn't going to force anything. He knew all about grief and the many methods of dealing with it. Or of not dealing with it.

She stirred on the blanket, and he helped her to her feet. She didn't glance at the cage, and he thought her voice was a bit overly bright when she said, "I want him to have a proper burial. Probably this afternoon between performances. Some spot that's quiet and peaceful."

"We'll see to it, Rachel," he assured her.

"Yes."

She got her bag, and he followed her from the tent.

There was a bloom on the grass as pale as frost when they emerged from the big top. But a rising sun, just clearing the distant treetops, was already beginning to burn the dew away. They stood outside the back door, blinking at the glare that was so unexpected after the gloom of the tent.

"There should be fresh coffee by now at the cookhouse," she suggested. "Maybe even breakfast is ready, if you're interested."

Craig glanced at her standing beside him. He wasn't hungry, and he wasn't sure he wanted more coffee. But he didn't think he could go back to his motel and try to sleep, either. Besides, he sensed her need not to be alone just yet.

"Sounds good," he agreed.

They started in the direction of the cookhouse tent, and then she stopped him. "Wait. I should look in on the mare first. Want to come with me?"

He shook his head. "I'll wait for you in the cookhouse."

He watched her head for the tent known as horse tops, and then he went on to the cookhouse truck and got two mugs of steaming coffee from the kitchen staff. They wanted to know about Napoleon and looked very sober when he told them. A loss was taken seriously on the circus, even if it was an old and ailing chimpanzee. Craig was beginning to understand that.

The picnic tables were deserted. None of the others was up yet. He sat at the edge of the tent and sipped his scalding coffee. He was bleary-eyed and unshaven, but the coffee and the crisp morning air revived him after the staleness of the big top.

Rachel joined him a moment later. She was smiling when she settled opposite him and reached for her mug. "We have a healthy new filly," she reported.

He smiled back at her over the rim of his mug, understanding her gladness. The birth of the foal was an eloquent evidence that life renews the cycle and eases suffering. Or, anyway, that was how it was supposed to work. But for him, that cycle had stalled.

They were silent as they drank their coffee, and then Rachel said shyly, "I want to thank you for being there with me all night, Craig. It meant a lot having your support." He would never know just how much it did mean to her. She couldn't tell him, for instance, that the touching image of a brash-mannered, rugged ex-marine singing a soothing lullaby to a frightened chimpanzee was a positive memory that she would cherish out of a situation that was otherwise sorrowful.

She had been restrained in her gratitude, thinking he might not welcome the recognition. Maybe this was so, because he merely nodded and said nothing.

Rachel watched him thoughtfully as he absently swirled the coffee in his mug. He looked so distracted, like a stranger again, and after the closeness they had shared during the long night, she couldn't bear this. She didn't want to lose their sense of togetherness. That was why she found the courage to tell him what had been at the back of her mind throughout the whole ordeal. That was why she reached out to him with a sudden, deliberate, "You know what it's like to lose someone who matters, don't you, Craig? You've experienced it yourself, haven't you?''

It had to be true, she thought. Craig Hollister hadn't always been the complete loner he pretended to be. There had to have been someone special in his world who had been cruelly snatched away from him. Otherwise, he wouldn't have been capable of the sensitive compassion he had demonstrated all night long. Yes, he knew about the deep pain of separation. She would swear to that.

Craig's gaze came up from his mug. He stared at her sharply, shocked by her bold perceptiveness. A familiar panic gripped him. He wanted to bang the mug on the table, leap to his feet and rush away. But he fought the urge, and it was a moment before he understood his resistance. And then he did grasp it.

He, too, had been remembering their harmony in the big top, had been as reluctant as Rachel to let it go. And there was something else. There was the long, aching emptiness he could no longer bear, the disgust with his old inability to trust affection and sympathy when it was offered, just because he'd always feared another rejection, another failure. If he valued what they had found in each other last night, if he wanted to preserve and maybe even expand on it, then he had to stop running away. He had to trust Rachel with the truth. It was time to rid himself of his long self-punishment.

At first, she was afraid he was clamping down on his emotions again, refusing the opportunity to confide in her. He was silent for a long time, his expression wary. Then, to her relief, he leaned toward her, propping his elbows on the old-fashioned red-and-white-checkered oilcloth covering the table.

"Yeah," he said, his voice husky with emotion. "Yeah, I do know what it's like to lose someone who matters. In fact," he added with a bitter smile, "you might say I'm an expert on the subject."

He paused and she waited patiently for him to go on. She guessed how difficult this was for him, that it must be something he rarely, if ever, talked about. She would have to give him time to tell it in his own way and at his own pace.

"I was lying, Rachel," he said finally, "when I let you think that I never cared that much about things like family and relationships with commitment. For most of my life, I even lied to myself about it. When I went into the marines right after high school, I was happy about it. For the first time in my life, I had something that gave me purpose and direction. I was good at being a marine. And who needed a family? The marines were my family."

"But it wasn't enough," she said insightfully.

"No," he admitted, "it wasn't enough. Deep down, I wanted something else. I wanted what I'd never had. I just—well, I just never knew how to go about finding it. Maybe I was afraid to look for it. You know, because of my childhood. Or maybe—" he said with a shrug "—just because that's the way I'm built. I was lucky, though, Rachel. I was damn lucky, because in the end, it found me. For a while, I had it all. I just didn't have the sense to hang on to it."

He broke off suddenly, looking uneasy. "Look, do you want more coffee? I can get us refills. Or what about something to eat? I think they were making scrambled eggs."

It was a stall tactic and she wasn't going to let him use it. Whether he realized it or not, he needed to release the anger and bitterness of his heartache, to get it all out. She shook her head slowly. "No coffee and no eggs. Go on," she said encouragingly, "tell me what you found, Craig."

He did understand that he needed to let it out. She could see that in the resigned way he lowered his arms, folding his hands on the tabletop. She could hear it in the determined quality of his voice as he made himself continue.

"It was Lynn who found me."

The someone who had mattered, Rachel realized, knowing she was about to hear something deeply distressing and that she had to have the courage to listen without emotional interference.

"She was a civilian on the base where I was stationed. I used to invent excuses to go into the office where she worked just so I could look at her. She was something. Hell, half the guys on the base were in love with her, including a couple of top-ranking officers. With that competition, I didn't think I stood a chance. Lynn saw it differently. She was the one who first asked me out."

"And you went."

"Yeah," Craig said, smiling in memory, "I went. And it was good between us right from the start. It didn't surprise Lynn. She knew how it was going to turn out for us. She always knew her own mind. Mine, too, most of the time. God, I was happy."

"She—she sounds like someone very special."

"She was. And so was our son."

Rachel stared at him, not as struck by this stunning disclosure as she was saddened by his use of the past tense. *Was.* He said *was* when referring to them. "You are—were a father?"

"And a husband." She caught the bleakness in his eyes before he lowered his gaze. For a moment, he studied his tightly folded hands on the tabletop. "I left the marines after Lynn and I were married," he said. "She was perfectly willing to be a marine wife, but I didn't want the corps anymore. I was suddenly ambitious. I wanted something I thought was bigger and better for my family, something with more money. I didn't want my son, David, growing up without the things I'd never had. The job offer in St. Louis came along and I took it. The thing is, I'd acquired this workaholic attitude in the marines, and that stayed with me in civilian life. I guess I needed to prove that the kid who'd been abandoned in a Pittsburgh tavern could amount to something. But Lynn understood that, so all the extra hours I spent on the job weren't a problem. At least not until—''

He broke off, his mouth suddenly hard, his eyes hollow with misery. His whole body had turned rigid and still. All but his hands. The interlocked fingers on the tabletop were flexing and unflexing in a slow, rhythmic desperation.

· "Until what?" she prompted gently.

At first, she didn't think he could bear to finish it, but finally, he made himself tell her. "Last fall," he said, his voice raw now with anguish. "We were finally going on that vacation I'd been promising Lynn ever since Davey was born, just the three of us. She'd been looking forward to it all summer. We were going to fly to Denver and rent a car, drive up into the mountains where we could see the first fall colors. Lynn was an orphan like me, but she did have this cousin who had a resort out there. We were going to spend a few days with the cousin and her husband.

"We got to Denver, all right, but I couldn't forget the damn job. There was this small electronics firm that I was advising. I was worried about their situation. I couldn't stand not calling from the airport to check on them. Well, they'd gotten themselves into another crisis, wanted to know if I could come back right away to straighten them out. A sensible man would have refused. I didn't. I agreed. Lynn was furious. We had a fight about it right there in the airport. I finally made her take the rental car and go on with Davey. I promised I would catch up with them at her cousin's. Just a day or two. I didn't want her vacation spoiled."

The emotion left Craig's voice. His words became brittle and flat, as if only in this mechanical way could he endure telling her the rest. "That was the last time I ever saw them, driving away from the airport. Lynn got to the mountains, all right. But there was an early snowstorm up there. She tried to get through to her cousin's. She was a good driver, but the road was bad. She lost control of the car. It went into a deep ravine. They never stood a chance. They were both killed.

"It could have been different if Lynn hadn't been using poor judgment because she was upset with me. It could have been different if I'd been at the wheel where I belonged instead of back in St. Louis, obsessed with business. That's what I've had to tell myself every day since I lost them. That's what I've had to try to live with."

Rachel, sharing his pain, felt as though a hand was squeezing her heart. "Craig," she whispered, appealing to him plaintively, "you can't be sure that any of that would have made a difference. You weren't there in the car. You don't know what actually happened."

He acted as though he hadn't heard her. Or probably, he had listened to this same argument before, maybe even from himself, and it hadn't helped. So why should he hear it again? "You know how I handled it all afterwards?" he said with a dry, ironic laugh. "I turned right around and made the same mistake all over again. I became even more of a workaholic. There weren't enough hours in the day to spend on the job. How's that for dealing with guilt?"

"I—I would say that, under the circumstances, it was probably a normal reaction."

"That's what they told me in grief counseling." He noted her surprise. "Oh, yeah, I tried that, too. Hank Sutherland insisted on it. They said I was working like a machine because I didn't want to give myself time to stop and confront my grief, that I was punishing myself because I was alive and my family wasn't. Hell, maybe they were right. All I knew was that I had to keep driving myself."

Rachel looked at his hands. They were clenching now on the tabletop in a kind of self-rage. She longed to touch those strong hands, to hold them comfortingly, to draw off all his massive torment. But she didn't think this was the right moment. Not yet.

Craig went on, his voice gruff again with feeling. "Finally, Hank and some other friends stepped in. They'd been watching me self-destruct all those months after the funeral. They—they said I was burned out, heading for a real collapse. I told them they were crazy."

Rachel could see how reluctant he was to admit his near breakdown. A tough ex-marine in the prime of his life didn't have nervous breakdowns. He'd been too hard on himself. All along, he'd been too hard on himself, failing to accept his human frailties.

"I refused to take a leave of absence," he said. "That's when Hank ordered me on this circus assignment. It was supposed to get me away from all the corporate stress, put me in a healthy outdoors situation with lighter demands. I wasn't given any choice about it." He smiled wryly. "So what do I do the other morning when Hank stops by to look me over? Am I grateful because he's worried about me? Oh, no, bastard that I am, I go and snap at the poor guy."

Rachel understood now what the banker had been trying to tell her. She was beginning to understand a lot of things, like the look on Craig's face that first time he'd arrived on the lot. Taut and serious, a man under a perpetual strain. He'd worn that look on other occasions, too, though he'd carefully hidden away the worst symptoms of his mental turmoil deep inside himself, where they'd festered like a poison. But now he had unburdened himself, so there was the hope— Wait. There was more, wasn't there? He hadn't finished it. And she hadn't learned it all.

"That day here with Susi," she said hesitantly, "when she brought you the cake..."

"Yeah. Well, things did get better with time, Rachel. I mean, the worst really did soften for me, but sometimes, when I'm around kids—"

"You can't handle it."

The more
you love romance . . .
the more
you'll love this offer

FREE!

Mail this heart today! (See inside)

Join us on a Silhouette® Honeymoon
and we'll give you
4 Free Books
A Free Victorian Picture Frame
And a Free Mystery Gift

IT'S A
SILHOUETTE HONEYMOON—
A SWEETHEART OF A FREE OFFER!
HERE'S WHAT YOU GET:

1. Four New Silhouette Desire® Novels—FREE!

Take a Silhouette Honeymoon with your four exciting romances—yours FREE from the Silhouette Reader Service™. Each of these hot-off-the-press novels brings you the passion and tenderness of today's greatest love stories…your free passports to bright new worlds of love and foreign adventure.

2. Lovely Victorian Picture Frame—FREE!

This lovely Victorian pewter-finish miniature is perfect for displaying a treasured photograph. And it's yours FREE as added thanks for giving our Reader Service a try!

3. An Exciting Mystery Bonus—FREE!

You'll be thrilled with this surprise gift. It is useful as well as practical.

4. Free Home Delivery!

Join the Silhouette Reader Service™ and enjoy the convenience of previewing 6 new books every month delivered right to your home. Each book is yours for only $2.49* each, a saving of 30¢ each off the cover price per book— and there is no extra charge for postage and handling. It's a sweetheart of a deal for you! If you're not completely satisfied, you may cancel at any time, for any reason, simply by sending us a note or shipping statement marked "cancel" or by returning any shipment to us at our cost.

5. Free Newsletter!

You'll get our monthly newsletter, packed with news about your favorite writers, upcoming books, even recipes from your favorite authors.

6. More Surprise Gifts!

Because our home subscribers are our most valued readers, when you join the Silhouette Reader Service™, we'll be sending you additional free gifts from time to time—as a token of our appreciation.

START YOUR SILHOUETTE HONEYMOON TODAY—
JUST COMPLETE, DETACH AND MAIL YOUR FREE-OFFER CARD

"Not that day. Not when Susi grinned up at me like that. It just hit me, remembering how Davey—" He stopped and shook his head regretfully.

"And—and Lynn? Do you still miss her terribly?" The instant the question was out of her mouth, Rachel hated herself for asking it, for *needing* to ask it. "I'm sorry," she apologized quickly. "That was a thoughtless, insensitive thing for me to ask. Of course, you miss her. You must miss both of them deeply."

"No, it was a fair question." He was thoughtful for a second, then told her honestly, "They'll always be a part of me, Rachel. I can't change that, but I think you have the right to know that emotionally, I have let Lynn go. I had to or I wouldn't have survived at all. I think I was able to do it because I realized in the end that she would have wanted it that way. But there is something I haven't managed, and I won't lie about it. What I do miss, always, every day, is the togetherness we had."

And that, Rachel realized, was the core of his despair. He had been harshly deprived of what had come to mean everything to him, and he had found no replacement for it. Perhaps he was even convinced he wasn't worthy of winning it again. But he was wrong about that. He was so very wrong. He was a decent man, strong in all the ways that mattered and deserving of what he needed. She wanted to tell him that, but she couldn't. Instead, she'd have to show him.

It was time. Time to obey her longing to reach out and touch him. She didn't have to say anything. All she had to do was make contact, let him know she was here for him. Words weren't necessary because he must have heard them all by now from his friends and in those grief counseling sessions. The only comfort he required in this unhappy moment was her silent understanding, her reassurance.

Her hands stretched across the table, covering the pair of big hands that were still locked in mindless combat on the tabletop. His knuckles were white with tension. She squeezed them gently, willing him to feel how much she cared.

For a moment, he didn't respond, but she kept her hands firmly on his. In the end, her unspoken message to him got through. With relief, she could feel the awful tension in him subsiding, his hands relaxing their grip on each other. She heard him expel a long, slow breath and knew he was releasing his worst pain.

Craig met her gaze, offering her a tremulous smile. He couldn't believe it! He actually felt at peace with his inner chaos for the first time since Lynn and Davey had been taken from him. He accepted it. Maybe now he could begin to deal with it, learn to put it behind him. Maybe he was going to be all right.

Rachel had done that for him, just by listening, just by caring. She was good for him. He wanted to let her know that.

She felt his hands turning insistently under hers. And suddenly, she was no longer clasping his hands. *His* were grasping *hers* in another wordless communication.

Bending toward her, he carried her fingers to his mouth, kissing them tenderly. Not in passion but in a simple, sweet gratitude that she found deeply moving.

And then she saw the teaspoon on the table in front of him. It had been trapped under his hands. The sight of it shocked her. He had punished the hard metal, twisted it under the force of his violent emotions. The battered spoon conveyed a sudden doubt she didn't want. If his feelings were that intense, still that raw, was she making a fatal mistake? Was she beginning to fall in love with a man who didn't know that he was perhaps still in love with the wife he had lost?

Six

Craig gazed in amazement at the sober crowd gathered in the field behind the circus lot. There wasn't a member of the company, performers and workers alike, who didn't want to be present for Napoleon's burial. They had come to honor a cherished friend. It didn't matter that he had been a chimpanzee. The event was being treated with the dignity and care of a family funeral. Craig thought he should have found the situation ludicrous, but he didn't. He actually understood it.

Rachel's wish had been observed. The spot selected for the grave was a serene one in a grove of stately oaks. The farmer who owned the land had given his permission for the burial.

Two of the men from the show had secured a small crate from town, and Molly had lined and covered it with fabric from the wardrobe trailer. The casket she had fashioned waited now over the grave, a bouquet of wildflowers resting on its lid.

For once, Craig realized, he didn't look out of place in his business suit. Every one of them had taken the trouble to dress in their best street clothes, all but the band, who were wearing their uniforms and carrying their instruments. In other respects, he felt distinctly uneasy. Rachel had particularly asked him to stand beside her directly in front of the grave. He hadn't objected, but now he wondered if her request wasn't a mistake. No one said anything, but he could feel them eyeing him, as if they thought his position was a presumptuous one. He didn't know that Rachel was intentionally keeping him at her side, that she was telling her people she wasn't going to have him excluded any longer from her circus family. She feared, however, that her determination wasn't enough by itself to win his acceptance.

Felix, deliberately avoiding Craig's gaze, signaled to her from the other side of the grave with a low, "Everybody's here now, Rachel."

She nodded. There was a long moment of silence as they waited for her to make the circus's farewell to Napoleon. A breeze rustled the oak leaves overhead, and afternoon heat shimmered in the meadow below.

Craig, as expectant as the others, glanced at Rachel and was worried. Except for those brief naps during the long night, she hadn't slept. There were tired smudges under her eyes, and she looked nervous. As far as he knew, she had yet to express any real grief for Napoleon. She hadn't shed a tear, which would have been natural, considering her love for the animal. She had kept it all inside, and he knew how wrong that was.

Rachel cleared her throat and started to speak. "Anyone who wasn't in the circus and saw us come together here like this would probably think we're a little crazy. They wouldn't understand that Napoleon wasn't just a chimpanzee to us, that he—he was—" She faltered, then made herself go on. "Well, he was special. He was of the circus, one of us, and—"

She stopped again, choking on her words. They were all watching her, waiting patiently for her to continue. It was ridiculous, but she just couldn't do this! She wasn't going to be able to manage the goodbye Napoleon deserved. The full realization of his loss had waited until this moment to overwhelm her. It all came rushing in on her at once: the knowledge that she could never again confide her private heartaches to Napoleon when no one else would do; that he could never again be the favorite playmate of her childhood; that she would never again see those intelligent old eyes gazing up at her lovingly.

She *was* being ridiculous! She could cry for Napoleon afterward. Right now, he was entitled to her tribute. She struggled on. "But you all know that. You know that h-he—" It was no use. Her throat had tightened up until she was croaking, and the silly tears were blurring her vision, threatening to become actual sobs. She was about to make an absolute emotional fool of herself!

Craig wasn't going to allow that to happen. As inconspicuously as possible, one of his arms slid around her waist, pressing her in support against his side. He astonished himself as much as he astonished the others when he quietly, smoothly took Rachel's place. No one stopped him. They were all too surprised. But Felix glared at him from across the grave, and there were mutters of displeasure elsewhere as he began to speak to them in his deep, resonant voice.

"There's an old saying in the circus. I know about it because I've heard some of you use it. I'm talking about the expression, 'Being with it and for it.' It refers to a circus trouper's loyalty to a show. I think that traditional saying is pretty appropriate here, because Napoleon was as much a circus trouper as any other.

"Maybe I have no right to be making this eulogy. I'm an outsider, after all. But I was with Rachel when Napoleon died. She confided some memories about him that made me understand just how entitled he is to this ceremony. They're pretty impressive credentials for a circus trouper. For those of you young enough not to know them, and for those of you who just want to remember, I'd like to share a few of them now...."

As Craig talked on, confidently praising Napoleon while he continued to hold Rachel close to him, a remarkable metamorphosis occurred among the mourners. The dark looks they directed at him, thick with the resentment they had felt for him since his first day on the lot, softened as they listened to his deep-felt sentiments. By the end of his tribute, without exception, they were regarding him not just with respect, but with wholehearted approval. Unintentionally, he had won their support.

Rachel wept quietly at his side, not just because she felt the change in her people and was moved by it, and not just because of Napoleon. It was because this big man, his arm protectively around her, had cared enough to rescue her from her own humiliation. If she hadn't been certain how she felt about him before, she was sure now.

There was no time to examine that feeling. Craig finished speaking, and after a moment of silent observance, the band began softly playing. It was a spirit-lifting circus song that had once accompanied Napoleon's bicycle act, but so bittersweet was the rendition that the entire gathering was misty eyed before the last notes faded away on the summer breeze.

The following morning, when the circus located on a new stand in western Ohio, the automatic stake driver quit on them in the first stages of raising the big top. Ernie, talented mechanic though he was, was unable to coax the temperamental machine back to life. It would need extensive repairs. If the show was to play its afternoon performance—and it couldn't afford not to—then the tent stakes would have to be driven by hand.

Craig, his customary briefcase tucked under his arm, arrived from his motel in time to witness the operation. Standing near the stake line marked out on the lot, he watched teams from the work crew rhythmically pounding the vital stakes.

Felix, directing the setup, sauntered to Craig's side. He didn't say anything for a minute. Then, tugging at his fedora and removing the perennial cigar from the corner of his mouth, he challenged Craig in a gruff voice. "You gonna stand there and just look, or you gonna dig in and help?"

In silence, Craig regarded the sweating teams. He understood that this old-fashioned method of burying the stakes in tough earth was a grueling, physically demanding business. A smile hovered at the corners of his mouth as he answered Felix. "Is that an order or an invitation?"

Felix grinned. "Invitation. Unless you're afraid of soiling those pretty duds you're always wearing."

Craig said nothing. He stripped off his suit jacket and tie, deposited them with his briefcase in the grass, rolled up his shirt sleeves, and helped himself to one of the sixteen-pound sledges waiting in the back of the canvas truck. Felix, watching him join one of the teams who welcomed him without a word, grunted in satisfaction.

Craig didn't need to be told that this was Felix's way of accepting him. The labor of driving the stakes was brutal, but no effort ever pleased him more.

On another lot in central Indiana, Molly came to him, her dainty face puckered in worry. "I don't know what we're going to do. We're short one of our candy butchers for tonight's performance."

Craig knew by now that "candy butcher" was a circus term for the individuals who hawked all the assorted refreshments in the big top. He also realized that this produced an important revenue for the show. "What happened?"

"Wayne. He's sick as a dog. He knows he's not supposed to eat shellfish. He has terrible reactions." She hesitated. "Craig, I hate to ask it, but there isn't anyone else available, so do you suppose just for tonight . . ."

Molly would never have considered asking such a favor of him before Napoleon's burial. None of them would have. He regarded her request as a compliment. He found himself that evening in the traditional white coat of a candy butcher, soda tray suspended from his neck as he circulated through the big top, offering his wares. He didn't consider the experience demeaning or embarrassing. He found it satisfying.

On a stand in northern Kentucky, he was helping to guy out the lines for the menagerie tent when Precious joined him. By now, Craig needed no invitation to pitch in wherever he was needed. The burly workman squatted at his side, watching Craig as he nimbly tied off the double half hitch that was the basic knot for circuses.

Precious offered him a wink and a toothless grin. "You got that down like a pro. Guess you're no longer a First of May, huh?"

Craig smiled back at him. "First of May? Haven't heard that one before."

"Sure. It's what we call the guys who are green when they join up at the start of a season. You ain't green now. Hey, when we're through here, some of us are gettin' up a poker game outside the bunkhouse truck. You wanna sit in?"

He did. It was one more evidence of his acceptance in the family.

The circus swung back into Illinois, Rock Island and Moline this time, and a long spell of hot weather. The high tide of summer. Even the early mornings were warm.

Rachel had just finished rehearsing the liberty horses and was watching the big top being assembled. Actually, what she was watching was Craig helping to ready the big top. At this initial stage of the setup, the canvas lay in flat sections on the ground, like pieces of a great pie. He was crouched over the canvas along with the rest of the men, rapidly lacing the pieces together.

The sight of him took her breath away. He was wearing a pair of snug cutoff jeans. The material was ragged and stained, his tennis shoes were scuffed and one had a hole in the toe. Shirtless, Craig's brawny chest was slick with sweat as he labored at the canvas. His tangled hair was also damp with perspiration. It looked shaggy around his ears, in need of a cutting. He didn't seem to notice or mind. The sun had bleached it until it was almost white in places, like his eyebrows. Hair and eyebrows made a vivid, tantalizing contrast against the deep, healthy tan he had acquired in just a matter of days. Rachel had found him appealing from the start, but in this rugged state, there was an aura of sexuality about him that was downright blatant. She didn't think she could stand it, not when—

"Amazing, isn't it?"

Her thought interrupted, Rachel brushed a tendril of hair away from her cheek and turned to find Ray Ford standing beside her. "What?"

"Him." The ringmaster nodded toward Craig, who was so busy concentrating on his task that he wasn't aware of them observing him. "I mean, when you look at him now, it's hard to remember the immaculate image that guy wore like a grudge. Now there's no job too dirty or menial for him, and he's actually cheerful about it. Guess that's the result of no longer being on the outside."

Rachel didn't say anything. She went back to watching Craig. Sweat was dripping from him, his upper-arm muscles bulging as he strained to lift a side pole into position. There was no evidence in that robust male form of the mental breakdown that had threatened him a few short weeks ago. She could feel the ringmaster waiting for her response. "Yes," she agreed quietly, "he is a changed man."

Ray, as perceptive as always, sensed there was something bothering her. "What is it, Rachel? I thought this was what you wanted, to have him accepted."

"It is," she said quickly. "It's been good for him, just what he needs. I am happy for him."

She didn't think Ray entirely believed her, but he didn't argue about it. After a moment, he walked away, leaving her alone again. Rachel went on standing there, angry with her frustration and the desire that was responsible for it.

The sight of Craig went on taunting her. She remembered picking up a towel yesterday he had used and then discarded after wiping the sweat off his hairy chest. She had secretly carried the towel back to her trailer where she'd sensually rubbed it against her cheek, sniffed at its nubby texture. It had still been warm from him and bore his distinctive odor. Not the woodsy after-shave he used with his business suits, but the pure scent of his own body, lusty and masculine. An ordinary towel! She was a fool! A *lovesick* fool!

She couldn't help it. She wanted him. It frightened her just how much she wanted him, because her feelings for him had intensified since that morning in the cookhouse tent. That morning when she had been startled by the realization that she must be falling in love with him. After the emotional intimacy they had shared then, she had hoped that a physical closeness would follow. After all, Craig had wanted her that night in his motel room. Why shouldn't he be eager to make love to her now when the conflict between them had been eased, when the situation was so right for a new togetherness? But it hadn't happened. He hadn't sought it. He was so busy being familiar with her circus family that he scarcely had a moment for her, and when he did . . .

Something was wrong. She could feel it. And she tried to understand it. He had been vulnerable that night at the motel when he'd reached out for her. He had overcome that vulnerability. Was that the difference? Had she, by helping to free him from his pain and confusion, made him think that it would be a mistake to become physically involved with her now that they knew and cared for each other on a deeper level? Ironic if so, but it could be the explanation. He might fear hurting her if he felt that some essential part of him still belonged to his wife, or if he had convinced himself that ultimately he couldn't stop being a loner unable to commit. Because no matter how warm his relationship was with her people these days, he would know the situation wasn't permanent. He would realize he had to move on again, maybe very soon. His life wasn't here. Hers was. And there lay the difference. And the despair.

Was it so hopeless? Was there no chance of their ever belonging to each other? She should talk to him about it. She should just go to him and openly discuss it, learn what he was feeling. But she couldn't bring herself to do that. Not just yet, anyway. She didn't want to spoil his newfound contentment with her family. He deserved that after his long, lonely exclusion.

Later, she promised herself as she turned and started for her trailer.

Craig was far from being immune to Rachel as he saw her walking away, her alluring hips swaying with an unconscious enticement that had his insides churning and his thoughts turning in an earthy direction. He had noticed her watching him. He had even guessed what she was feeling. There had been an unmistakable yearning on her face. And, damn it, he wanted her as much as she wanted him! Then what was holding him back?

He didn't know. His emotions were all mixed up and he couldn't seem to sort them out. And that didn't make sense, either, when, for the first time in months, he felt like a whole man again. No longer isolated in his old cynicism, he slept without interruption every night. And his days were filled with hard physical work and an easy camaraderie he hadn't known since the marines. He was grateful for that, pleased that he was learning to value the devotion of these people to one another, the simple loyalty and hardiness that had them daily battling the elements to keep the circus going.

Whether they realized it or not, they had given him something very precious. They had given him the chance to begin healing himself. Whether this slow process would ever rid him of his old insecurities, he didn't know. There was still that desire deep inside him for a real family and the conviction he wasn't meant to have it. It was a longing that events had taught him to mistrust. He was a man afraid to love again because he might lose again.

Was this, then, the explanation for his resistance to Rachel? Why he struggled against the intimacy his body craved? Certainly his longings were complicated now by his deeper feelings for her. She represented everything that had been unattainable for him, and if he involved himself with her, if he became her lover... No, he didn't think he was capable of risking it. It wasn't safe.

Besides, there was another obstacle to contend with. Her overprotective circus family. Though they might have accepted him on one level, they were still suspicious of his intentions where Rachel was concerned. Craig didn't know if those watchful ranks would appreciate it if he and Rachel were to become lovers right under their noses. Not that there was ever a real opportunity for that, anyway. He and Rachel never seemed to find themselves alone these days.

All that changed when the circus's route brought them deep into Wisconsin and Rachel needed him at her side in a desperate situation.

"It's the radiator," Rachel explained to Felix. "Ernie thinks I probably need a new one."

"What you need is a new car," Felix grumbled.

"I can afford to replace the radiator, not the car. Anyway," she said, defending the station wagon that had been her father's, along with the house trailer it pulled, "it's perfectly dependable, thank you."

"So, what's the plan?"

"I've already called a garage here. They'll take care of me. You go on with the others. I'll catch up."

"You sure?"

"Felix, I'll be fine. It will probably take a couple of hours, so don't look for me at the new stand before noon. Nothing to worry about when we're not scheduled to play again until tomorrow."

"Well, you be careful. The forecast is for rain today, maybe heavy rain."

"I will," she promised.

The rural Wisconsin lot where Donelli's Circus had played the day before was largely emptied of the show's vehicles when Rachel headed into the adjacent town. The long trucks had pulled out just after daybreak, and the performers' rigs had begun to follow soon after that. Due to modern traffic, the circus never traveled in a caravan as it had in former days.

Rachel scanned the parking lot as she passed the highway motel where she knew Craig had spent the night. His car wasn't there. She figured he must have gone on to the next stand to be on hand for the new setup. It was unreasonable of her, but it gave her a lonely feeling realizing he wasn't close by. Only how could she miss what she'd never had?

Her mood was probably due to the weather, she decided as she eyed the threatening sky from the window of the garage while she waited for her car to be repaired. The weather had been clear and hot for days, but now it looked like it was going to break. The temperature was already noticeably cooler. Like farmers, circus troupers were always conscious of the weather. Extremes meant bad gates or lots too wet and muddy for proper setups.

It was raining long before Rachel's car was finished. By the time she left the garage and regained the highway, the rain was falling in a steady downpour. Since this was farm country she was traveling, with a lot of uninhabited state forest lands, there was little traffic to deal with. But pulling the heavy house trailer behind her was never easy, and she had to drive slowly enough not to miss the arrows that were posted at crucial intervals along the route. They were difficult to spot through the driving rain.

Gypsy Jack, Donelli's band leader and advance man, was responsible for the arrows. It was his job to tack them up on posts and trees ahead of the show in order to guide them safely through unfamiliar territory to the next lot. It was called "railing the route," from the days when advance men borrowed rails from farmers' fences to mark turnings for the old traveling wagon shows.

Rachel almost missed the blue arrow where the highway paused at a stop sign before it continued on after a sharp right. When she did finally see the arrow on the side of an abandoned shed, she was surprised. It pointed to the left.

She hesitated before deciding to obey it. She knew that sometimes, because of overpasses too low for the circus trucks or road work on the main highways, Gypsy Jack would detour the show over dependable side routes. She assumed this was the case here since the road to the left looked well paved.

She traveled only a few miles, however, before she grew suspicious. The road became narrower, scarcely two lanes in width, as it crawled through a dense pine forest. She kept looking for another encouraging blue arrow, but there was none.

This can't be right, she thought. Gypsy Jack would never have brought the trucks through here.

Drawing to the side of the road, she pulled out a map and consulted it. She had trouble even finding the minor route she was on. When she did finally locate it on the map, it was what she feared. The road seemed to go nowhere except deep into a vast state forest preserve.

The arrow back at the stop sign must have been altered after the show went through. It happened from time to time. Kids playing a prank, thinking it was funny to send the circus off on a dead-end.

She would have to return to the highway. But she needed a place to turn around, something spacious enough to accommodate both the station wagon and the house trailer. Backing all that distance was out of the question.

She went on, searching for an opening in the trees. But the ranks of pines, crowding in on both sides of the road, were unbroken. The road, if anything, got narrower. There wasn't a sign of life anywhere, no buildings, no other vehicles, no side lanes. All she had for company were the dismal pines and the cheerless rain that never quit.

Rachel was beginning to get worried when the road finally dipped, crossing a stream over a low earthen causeway. A pair of culverts carried the waters through the causeway, but the stream was so swollen with the torrents of rain that the drains couldn't carry off the excess fast enough. The waters were rapidly rising at the banks, endangering the roadway. But the pavement had yet to be flooded, so Rachel crossed the stream with caution.

She was glad she did. Just a short distance away on the other side, off to the left, was a clearing with a few picnic tables and a pair of primitive outhouses. Ah, a turnaround at last!

With care, she bumped off the road. The surface was mostly gravel, but she needed a wide swing in order to bring both car and trailer back onto the road. She thought she was achieving just that on ground that was still firm, until she hit mud. Treacherous mud. The right wheels of the station wagon sank into deep ooze.

Rachel spent several tense moments trying to ease out of the trap, but all she succeeded in doing was digging herself deeper. This was no good. The wheels were spinning uselessly in the slickness of the mud. She needed traction.

Exasperated with the situation, she reached for her rainwear in the back seat. She was out of the car in seconds and searching for branches and rocks to stuff under the tires.

Rachel must have spent close to an hour trying everything she could think of, including unhitching the trailer, in order to free the station wagon. Nothing worked. All she got for her efforts was very wet and very dirty. The rain was so heavy that not even her coat and plastic hood were enough to keep her dry. Or warm.

Miserable and discouraged, she realized she had only one choice. She would have to hike all the way back to the highway and find help.

Locking the car and trailer, she left the picnic grove and trudged along the roadway. When she came to the causeway, she stopped in dismay. She couldn't cross it. It was underwater now. Deep, powerfully racing water that would carry her with it if she tried to wade it.

She had to go back. She would need to follow the road in the opposite direction and pray that it would lead her out of here before darkness fell.

She turned around and retraced her steps. She passed the clearing, came around a bend and stopped again. A second causeway. This one was even more deeply submerged than the first. Another branch of the same stream rushed over it.

It was then, with a sense of awful panic, that Rachel understood her helpless dilemma. She was on an island! Stranded alone on a low island, with the wild waters threatening to engulf it!

Seven

No one on the new stand was thinking about Rachel. They were too busy dealing with one of the circus's worst nightmares—a soft lot with standing water. The relentless rain had turned the ground into a quagmire, making the pitching of the show a punishing operation.

There was no possibility of raising the big top, which wouldn't be needed until tomorrow, anyway. But the trucks and rigs couldn't be left on the road blocking traffic. They would have to be spotted somehow on the lot and the animals, at least, unloaded and settled. The forklift was useless under these conditions. That meant that the loads on the trailers had to be lightened by hand, with everyone on the show helping to carry in the essential equipment. The harnessed elephants also aided in the work. Even with all this, vehicle after floundering vehicle sank into the slop up to its axles and had to be rescued.

So much rope and chain were used in the towing and dragging that the supply ran short by early afternoon. Craig volunteered to drive into town to buy more.

The community wasn't a large one. There was only one hardware store and that was closed for the day because of a family wedding. He spent a frustrating half hour before he located a junk store with a quantity of secondhand rope. He wasn't in a good mood by the time he dumped the stuff into his trunk and returned to the circus. He was wet, caked with mud and tired from long hours of uninterrupted labor. He was also wondering about Rachel. He'd been so busy helping with this mess that he hadn't stopped to think about her. But now it occurred to him that he hadn't seen her all morning and usually, she was everywhere on the lot.

After delivering the rope to the work crew, Craig went searching for Felix. The cookhouse wasn't functioning, but Molly and Lucille had made coffee available in the office wagon. Felix was there with Ray, taking a break.

"Where's Rachel?" Craig demanded. "Didn't she get here from the last lot?"

Felix explained about the radiator.

Craig was angry. "Why didn't anyone tell me? If I'd known she was having car trouble, I would have stayed back and driven behind her to make sure she got here."

Felix for once was calm and casual, explaining patiently. "Takes a long time to replace a radiator, and this weather makes for slow driving. She'll get here. Rachel knows how to take care of herself."

Craig wasn't satisfied. He stamped off to look for a phone. He was back a short while later, reporting grimly, "I managed to get through to that garage. They said she left there long ago. She should have been here by now. So, where is she?"

Felix lowered his coffee cup and cleared his throat. "Well, maybe you're right. Maybe that old wagon of hers did start acting up again. Guess I'd better send a couple of the boys back that way to look for her.''

Whatever Craig felt for Rachel—and he had acknowledged to himself it was considerable—it had never been savage in any degree. Until now. His emotions went wild. "The hell you will!" he exploded. "You people have been so busy protecting her from me that you haven't stopped long enough to notice that the fool woman sometimes needs protection from herself! If anybody's going after her to haul her out of whatever mess she may have gotten herself into, it's going to be me! And," he added forcefully, glaring warningly at both men, "I wouldn't advise either one of you to object to that!"

There was silence in the trailer after Craig had banged out and headed for his car. Then Ray quietly observed, "Would you say the ex-leatherneck has gotten just a bit territorial about our Rachel?"

"Yeah, I sort of noticed that. Interesting development, huh? Think I should go along with him?"

"Uh, in his present state of mind, I wouldn't recommend it."

Felix nodded slowly. "Then I guess we've got us a little worrying here on our own until we hear from them and know they're okay. A real bitch of a day, isn't it?"

Craig never stopped to think why he had to go after Rachel. He just knew that he did and that if anything had happened to her, he'd never forgive himself.

He wanted to race down the highway to reach her, wherever she was, but he forced himself to drive slowly over the route. It was the only way he could search the roadsides for her car. He kept hoping to find her stalled on the shoulder, calmly waiting for help. But he knew if she'd had engine trouble, she would have walked to a phone somewhere and gotten a message to them. Only they hadn't heard from her.

That's what worried him. That's what made him absolutely sick with worry the farther he drove. This was a thinly populated region. There were few vehicles along the highway. If she'd had an accident, overturned in a deep ditch thick with high brush, it would be easy to overlook her in the torrents of rain. He could be missing her himself, even though he was carefully looking for her. She could be lying somewhere pinned in the wreckage, injured and unconscious.

He didn't want to think of his wife and son. He didn't want to remember how they had died and how he hadn't been there for them. He didn't want to compare this situation to their situation. But he couldn't help remembering. He couldn't stop fearing that it might be happening all over again, and if he lost Rachel like he'd lost Lynn and David... He couldn't stand it!

Craig was frantic by the time he reached the old lot. There was no sign of Rachel anywhere. The lot was deserted, looking forlorn in the falling rain. There would have been no reason for her to return here, but he hadn't wanted to overlook any possibility. God, where was she? *Where was she?*

He went to the garage where her radiator had been replaced. He was told all over again that she had left there hours ago. He used the phone and called the state police. The police informed him that there had been no accident involving a station wagon and house trailer. They assured him their highway patrols would be on the lookout for her. Craig said he would check back with them.

Why hadn't he installed that cellular phone in his car as he had been promising himself? It would make all of this easier. Why weren't the circus vehicles equipped with phones for emergencies just like this one? Not enough funds, of course. Well, he was going to recommend it in his next report, even if it meant he had to buy the damn phones out of his own pocket and wrap them around Rachel's proud, lovely neck.

What now? He couldn't just stand here. He had to do something. He got in his car and began to drive back over the route. It was late afternoon now. There wouldn't be many hours of daylight left, especially not with the skies so overcast.

Again, he carefully searched both sides of the highway. On the drive over, he hadn't thought about the arrows Gypsy Jack had posted. Anyway, they hadn't been facing him. Now they were. He saw it this time at the stop sign. The arrow straight ahead of him on the side of the old shed. The blue arrow pointing not to the right but to the left, down a side road. Had it been wrongly positioned like that when Rachel had come through?

Craig didn't hesitate. Swinging to the left, he sped off through the pine forest. When he came to the flooded causeway minutes later, he jerked to a stop and jumped out of his car. Had Rachel crossed here? It didn't seem possible with those deep, tearing waters. Her wagon would have stalled. But if the causeway hadn't been submerged when she passed this way...

How was he going to get over there? How was he going to follow her? He didn't doubt now that she was somewhere on the other side. Leaning in through the open car door, he laid on the horn. Maybe she would never hear it. Maybe she was miles away by now, possibly even back with the circus. But he kept sounding the horn, calling to her.

And then, trotting toward him through the trees on the other side of the causeway, came a figure. A familiar figure. He had never been so thankful in his life!

She waved her arms, shouting to him. He went down to the edge of the stream to talk to her. "Are you all right?" he called.

"I'm fine, but I'm caught here. It's an island, Craig. I didn't realize that when I came over, and then I got stuck in the mud when I tried to turn around and head back. I couldn't get the car out, and by the time I walked back to the causeway, it was all underwater like this. There's another causeway on the other side, and that's underwater, too. I've been trying to figure out what to do, because the water keeps rising and what if the island floods, and—"

"Easy, sweetheart, easy. We'll get you out."

"How? The current is too swift for wading. Oh, Craig—"

"I'm coming over for you."

"No! You can't!"

"Wanna bet? Just hang on."

He knew how he was going to manage it. He had a length of rope in the trunk of his car left over from his purchase at the junk store. There was only one problem. He hadn't given this particular coil of line to the work crew because it had looked too old and worn. Could he trust it now to bear his weight? He would soon find out.

Getting the rope and a heavy lug wrench from the car, Craig tied one end of the line around the weight of the wrench and the other around the trunk of a tree.

"Stand back, Rachel," he instructed her.

When she was in the clear, he cast the wrench over the causeway. It took several tries before he managed to land it in the roadway on the other side. Rachel scooped it up, released the wrench and snugged her end of the rope around another tree.

Now that there was a makeshift railing to hang on to, she felt confident about trying the causeway. She told Craig as much. "You don't have to cross. There's no point in that. I can—"

"No, you don't!" he ordered sharply. "You stay put!" He wasn't going to have her safety jeopardized by the questionable rope, not before he had tested it under his own weight.

"But—"

"No arguments!"

She gave him none after that. Secretly, she was pleased that he was coming for her and that he was handling the whole thing with old-fashioned, take-charge, male authority. She waited for him meekly, watching as he shed his shoes and socks, thrust them into his car and rolled up his pant legs.

"Be careful," she warned as he started to wade onto the flooded causeway. "The current looks awfully strong."

It *was* strong, he discovered as he worked his way across. The waters tugged at him powerfully. He was glad he had the line to cling to. He just hoped it wouldn't break under the strain.

Craig was nearly to the other side when the weakened rope snapped without warning. The recoil caused him to lose his treacherous footing. He would have tumbled into the racing stream if Rachel hadn't dashed forward into the shallow end and caught him around the waist to steady him. Together, they staggered out of the water, lost their balance on the slick pavement and collapsed onto the roadway.

Rachel suddenly found Craig sprawled on top of her. The pavement under her back was wet and cold. His weight crushed her into bits of sharp gravel, robbing her of her breath. But nothing had ever felt so right and wonderful as that solid body protectively covering hers.

She didn't care about the wet and cold or the painful gravel. She would have gone on happily bearing his compact body against hers if they hadn't been startled by a deep voice hailing them from across the causeway.

"You folks all right over there?"

Craig shifted away from Rachel, got to his feet and helped her to stand. There was a highway-patrol car parked next to Craig's blue sedan on the other side. The young officer belonging to it was standing at the edge of the water, watching them anxiously.

"We're fine," Craig assured him, and went on to explain what had happened.

"Yeah," the officer said, "these causeways are always flooding in heavy rains. County needs to do something about raising them. We had a party trapped on the island once before. That's why I came down now to check. Well, look, don't worry. The island itself never floods. But as a precaution, I'll get them to close a gate on the dam upstream. Thing is, the waters over the causeway here probably won't go down enough before dark. Means you'll either have to wait, or we'll have to figure some way to get you out."

"Not necessarily," Rachel said. She told him about her fully equipped trailer back in the picnic grove.

"That's all right, then. You got someplace warm and dry to sit it out. That being the case, best thing is to wait until morning. I'll come by early to make sure everything's okay for you. Anything I can do before then?"

Craig asked him to contact the circus and let them know he and Rachel were both safe. The officer promised he would and then departed. Things were looking up. Even the rain had dwindled to a thin drizzle.

Now that Craig was with her, Rachel wasn't concerned in the least. Everything was going to be fine. Or was it? He was suddenly silent as they trudged side by side toward the clearing where the trailer waited under the pines. She glanced up at him questioningly. His profile was like stone. What was wrong?

When they reached the clearing, she dug out her key and unlocked the trailer. He had said nothing since they'd left the causeway. She turned her head to ask him why and found him over by her car, glowering at the wheels sunk in the mud.

"Craig?"

His only answer was a muttered expletive that was probably standard marine vocabulary. She didn't press it. She went on into the trailer, shed her coat and hood, and kicked off her shoes. There was no outside electricity, of course, but the batteries and bottled gas fed a few lamps and the space heater. Both were welcome, and within minutes, the trailer was warm and cozy.

She was reaching for a pair of towels in a storage locker when Craig finally came into the trailer. She looked around, wanting to ask him if he thought they could free her car in the morning without calling a tow truck. She didn't ask that. He was standing there against the door, hands jammed into his pockets, a fierce scowl on his face.

Rachel left the towels and crossed to him. "You're angry with me," she said in realization. "Why?"

He glared at her, blue eyes hard, voice like a grizzly's growl. "Automatic stake drivers that can't wheeze through another season, patched tents, station wagons too old to be dependable, no communication equipment to contact each other in emergencies! It stinks!"

Her eyes went wide in bewilderment. "What? What are you—"

"And just look at you!" he roared, hands coming out of his pockets to gesture at her feet. "Your socks are soaked! Why haven't you changed them? Why haven't you gotten out of those wet clothes?"

She was a mess, he thought. Her long hair was tangled, there was a smudge of dirt on one cheek, and her blouse was coming out of her waistband. She was a sweet, beautiful mess, and he wanted to strangle her.

"Why can't you take care of yourself?" he bellowed. "Do you realize how sick with worry I was? You might have gotten yourself killed out there today! You might have—"

He couldn't go on. He was shaking with an uncontrollable emotion he didn't fully understand. And all she could do was stand there and stare at him out of those big green eyes that drove him crazy. He had to do something about that. He had to do something about her.

He did. With a wild groan, his arms went around her. He wasn't gentle about it, either. He was rough and furious and totally possessive as he hauled her against his length, crushing her with a tightness he wasn't yet prepared to recognize as gratitude and deep relief for the well-being of a woman who meant everything to him.

Rachel, breathless in his steel embrace, wasn't given the opportunity to point out to him that, as appearances went, he was in much worse shape than she was. Without the benefit of a raincoat, his sweatshirt and jeans were wet to the skin, his hair was plastered to his scalp and his feet were bare and dirty. Not that it mattered. He looked wonderful. He felt even better. Her heart, which was busy slamming against her ribs as he held her, told her as much.

His mouth told her more when it sloped over hers in a kiss as demanding as his arms. It was a marvelous kiss loaded with the heat and scent and flavor of him. Exactly the sort of kiss she had been wanting from him for days. A kiss that involved his yearning lips, his teasing, stroking tongue, his breath mingling intimately with hers.

All of Craig's earlier arguments to himself as to just why he shouldn't get physically involved with her fled in the face of her soft, lush appeal, her willing mouth under his. He couldn't remember a single one of those arguments. He didn't *want* to remember any of them.

He was trembling when his mouth finally lifted from hers. He rested his chin weakly against her brow, his voice gritty with need. "So, where were we?"

She drew back in the circle of his arms, summoning a shaky smile. "Beg pardon?"

"Before the whole thing got interrupted that night after Baraboo," he reminded her.

"Oh," she whispered. "I—I believe you were telling—*showing*—me your fantasies."

"Yeah." He grinned slowly in memory. "I think it had something to do with this."

His hands slid down her back, cupping her rounded bottom to pull her tightly against the hard ridge of flesh that was straining his jeans. He rubbed against her, thrusting toward the cradle of her womanhood to demonstrate his intention.

Rachel gasped at the rigid feel of him. "Craig—"

"Yeah, I know," he muttered, one of his hands reaching behind him to slap at the wallet in his back pocket. "Only this time, I'm carrying the protection on me. I wasn't going to risk any more interruptions."

"Just in case?" she asked, understanding his reference to that night in his motel when he had frantically searched for the misplaced condoms.

"Just in case," he agreed, knowing that if he had prepared in advance for the possibility of this moment, he couldn't have meant any of his careful arguments against it. Not ever.

"Then I would like to learn the rest of those fantasies," she said.

"To hell with fantasies," he told her impatiently, his voice a husky promise as she squirmed against him, destroying all his control. "Let's just wing it."

"Yes," she said. "Yes, please."

His hands shifted again, scooping her up into his arms. He meant to carry her to the bedroom at the back of the trailer. He never got any farther than the wide sofa a few paces away. He wanted her to belong to him in every way, and he couldn't wait.

He sank down onto the sofa, settling her snugly on his lap. He kissed her again, lingering over the tiny scar he loved at the corner of her mouth. And then he began to make his own brand of slow, profound love to her. He needed to touch her everywhere, know every portion of her.

He carried her hands to his mouth, the point of his tongue tracing their slimness, his teeth nipping gently at the folds of flesh between her fingers. He eased her out of her blouse, disposed of her bra and pleased his hands with the satin fullness of her breasts. He bent his head, his tongue laving one dusky aureole, then the other. He drew her pebble-hard nipples deep into his mouth.

Rachel arched against him, a pleading whimper low in her throat as she tangled her fingers in his thick hair.

"What, sweetheart?" he whispered. "What do you want? Tell me everything you want."

But she wasn't able to express her wants. It didn't matter. He knew exactly what she needed, and he planned to satisfy her every desire.

Her slacks were a barrier. He had to rid her of her slacks. He tugged at the elastic waistband. Understanding, she lifted herself to accommodate him. He dragged the slacks down over her long, shapely legs, depositing them on the floor along with her socks.

She would have lowered herself again onto his lap. He wouldn't let her. He kept her raised until her panties had followed the slacks, until she was freed of her last article of clothing. And then he nestled her onto his lap again, sighing with the pleasure of holding her like this, her flesh completely exposed to his gaze and his touch. She had a lovely body, her olive skin heated with a dark, seductive flush.

He could see her swallow with emotion before she spoke to him. "Aren't we going to—you know?"

"Yes," he assured her softly, "we're going to have it all."

"But *your* clothes—"

"We'll get to me in a minute, love."

She was shy with him because she was naked and he was still dressed. He liked her shyness. He liked everything about her. He wanted to show her how much he cared. He wanted to please her at the most meaningful level. He was going to do just that.

He supported her with one hand on her back, his other hand parting and stroking the inner flesh of her thighs. He could feel the sweet warmth spreading through her under his caressing fingers, could hear her breath quicken against his shoulder where her face was buried. His hand moved on until his fingers stirred through the nest of soft curls at the apex of her thighs. Until he found the source of her womanhood.

"Craig, what—"

"Shh," he hushed her. "Let me touch you. Let me make you feel how special you are."

She clung to him then with trust and new awareness as his hand tenderly parted her delicate petals. So wet, so tight. His fingers penetrated her depth with care, began moving inside her. A slow, steady rhythm.

She clenched at him with moans and little cries, her body writhing with mounting passion. He could feel the tension building in her as he increased the pressure on the nub of that moist, quivering flesh.

He sensed the approach of her release, and held on to her tightly as the first powerful spasms rocked through her body. Wave after wave swept over her, shocking her with the intensity of her climax until she was actually sobbing against him.

He went on holding her protectively until the long contractions subsided, until she was limp and quiet in his arms. He was delighted with her violent responses. Rachel was embarrassed, disbelieving.

"Craig, I didn't—I mean, I never before, *ever,* felt anything— Well, I don't know what happened to me."

He shushed her again, rocking her slowly. "There was nothing wrong about it, love. In fact, it was everything that was right."

"Yes," she said, thinking how caring and loving he was as her heart swelled with gratitude for him. She sighed and rested her head against his chest. He held her quietly, making no demands, allowing her a long moment of recovery. But when she shifted on his lap, she became aware of the rocky bulge in his jeans stirring against her naked skin, aching for relief.

Poor man. All this time he had been suffering without a complaint.

She wanted to please him then as he had pleased her. She wanted the ultimate fulfillment for both of them.

Her hands tunneled under his sweatshirt, her fingers sifting through the springy hair on his hard chest. She could feel his rapid heartbeat, and when she flicked his flat male nipples, she heard his breathing turn harsh with arousal.

"Your sweatshirt is damp," she accused him, imitating his earlier anger with her. "Why can't you take care of yourself?"

"Yeah?" He pushed her hands away and peeled the sweatshirt over his head, tossing it to the floor. "There. Better?"

"Let me see." Her face came down against his bare chest. She pressed kisses against his nipples, her tongue circling them slowly. His breathing grew even harsher. She went lower, her mouth reaching his navel imbedded in little whorls of dark gold hair. The tip of her tongue delicately traced the shape of his navel. He tasted wonderful. He was groaning now.

Rachel drew back. "No, not better. You've still got some wet clothes here to get out of."

The groan turned to a growl. He caught her around the hips and planted her on the sofa beside him. Coming to his feet, he paused only long enough to retrieve the packet from his wallet before he shucked off his jeans and briefs. Kicking them away, he faced her. "Satisfied?"

It was her turn to find breathing difficult as she viewed his awesome arousal. He was magnificent.

Craig sank beside her on the sofa, drawing her toward him, bringing her hands down against him. "Care to feel how I'm no longer damp and cold?" His invitation was deep and sexy.

Rachel couldn't resist it. Her fingers wrapped around his hardness, stroking down to gently fondle the vulnerable and precious life-giving sac it served.

"I don't think," he rasped, "that we'd better—"

"—Wait any longer," she finished for him.

"Oh, yeah."

She started to stretch back on the sofa, but he caught her wrist, pressing the packet into her hand. "Here," he whispered, "you do it."

"Craig, I don't—"

"Please. I want to feel you doing it for me."

She obeyed his request, slitting the packet and removing the condom. It was a totally new experience for her, but how difficult could it be? Well, tricky enough that her fingers trembled as she carefully, slowly unrolled the protection over his supersensitive length.

Craig shuddered, sucking in his breath sharply. "Easy, sweetheart, easy."

Rachel stopped. "Am I hurting you?"

"It's not that. It's—" How could he tell her that what she was doing was so absolutely sensual that if she went on doing it, he might not last through the process? Somehow, by exercising a massive restraint, he did manage it.

It was much less easy to preserve that restraint when, seconds later, she lay under him on the sofa, her body all warm and voluptuous and willing. He was ready to accommodate her. Ready? Hell, he'd been fully prepared for the past twenty minutes. It was time to alleviate his torment.

Gathering her in his arms, he permitted himself one long, reverent kiss. It was the only delay he could endure. Rachel, understanding his need, parted for him. Trembling with urgency, Craig eased himself slowly, steadily into the welcoming vessel of her body.

The silken sensation of her closing around him was incredible. He could feel himself swelling to new dimensions inside her. When their joining was fully achieved, he rested, wanting to savor the sweet fusion as long as possible.

"Oh, Rachel," he rumbled, "I've never felt anything so— *don't*—oh, don't rock like that, sweetheart, or I won't be able to—" The rest of his words were lost in a guttural groan.

He wanted to prolong their union. He did try. He really did. But Rachel's hips kept moving demandingly under his. He couldn't withstand the torture. He had to answer it with his own thrusts, slow and measured at first, then increasing in tempo, building to a frenzy.

With bodies clasped and straining, her limbs entwined around him to ensure a perfect oneness, they forged their pinnacles in a crucible of molten passion. The storm broke over them almost simultaneously, wild and raw and blindingly incandescent.

The tremors slowly dwindled, the roaring decreased, leaving in the storm's aftermath a calm, sweet glow. When her breathing had steadied, Rachel smiled up at him lovingly, her fingers stroking the contours of his face. He caught her hand, pressing an emotional kiss in the hollow of her palm. They didn't speak. Their bodies had expressed all that was necessary.

It was with deep reluctance that Craig drew away from her. But only in brief necessity to dispose of the protection. Then he settled beside her, cradling her in the circle of his arm. The sofa wasn't all that generous in width, but he kept her so close that they managed to just fit its space.

Steeped in contentment, her head against his shoulder exactly where he felt it belonged, Rachel drowsed. Craig didn't sleep. In the long, mellow silence that followed, his mind was busy.

His gaze roved the interior of the trailer—as much of it as he could see, anyway, from his prone position. Rachel had made it a snug, pleasant home for herself. There was comfortable seating and plenty of pillows in needlepoint covers. Photos were everywhere. Circus-family photos of faces beloved to her. A pair of shelves was loaded with prized trophies won in circus competitions, and the paneled walls were crowded with framed, old-time circus posters.

Everywhere the circus. And the circus people. The family she had offered to him because he hadn't one of his own and she had felt that he needed a family. She would never know how touched he was by that, by her simple, earnest caring from the heart. That was why he had to save her family for her. That was why he had to save the circus.

He thought about it carefully as he held her. Since Napoleon's burial, he had taken on a different role. He'd been so busy enjoying the warm camaraderie of the company, so occupied with discovering his new self through his daily activities with the show that he had forgotten why he was there. It had been days since he had devoted any attention at all to his real job.

It was time to get practical again, be the financial troubleshooter he was supposed to be. The season had been good, but the gates had not been consistently impressive. They needed to be if Donelli's Circus was ever to be profitable again.

There had to be a way of achieving this without sacrificing personnel. That was as unthinkable to him now as it was to Rachel. After all, by extension, they were his family, as well—though Craig had yet to fully believe in that miracle. He had trusted such relationships before, only to be cheated of them. Just the same, he wouldn't consider cutting jobs. He would need to find some other means of rescuing the ailing circus.

He concentrated on the problem for long minutes. Then he remembered something he had tucked away in the corner of his mind. Karl Dvorak, the pompous cat trainer, had been bragging to him one morning in the cookhouse tent about his success last season on a rival circus. The Czech was regretting that he hadn't signed on again with the other show. It played the same Midwestern circuit and was of a comparable size, but its attendance records this year were phenomenal. Ray Ford had reluctantly admitted this was true when Craig mentioned it to the ringmaster. Craig had done nothing about the information at the time. Now he would pursue it. He would pay a visit to that other circus and learn what they were doing that Donelli's was not doing.

He felt better now that he had decided on a course of action. When the dozing Rachel stirred in his arms, he lifted his head to gaze down tenderly at her peaceful face. His heart swelled in his chest with something that was both possessive and protective. He cared for this woman deeply. Maybe he wasn't ready to call it love. Maybe he didn't know where the feeling was going to take them. But whatever it was, it was genuine enough and strong enough to be the most vital reason of all for saving her circus.

Rachel roused herself a moment later and smiled at him sleepily. She started to slide away from him. His arm tightened around her, hugging her back to his side.

"Where do you think you're going?" he demanded.

"Just to—"

"No, you're not," he informed her gruffly. "You're staying right here."

She was going to have problems with this guy, Rachel decided. He was definitely the proprietary kind. She didn't mind, though. She didn't mind in the least.

Her warm, soft nearness aroused him. Craig wanted to make love to her again. And he did.

Eight

By the following morning the causeways were free of water. They were able to drive off the island and return to the circus lot. That was when Craig told her he would need to be gone for a couple of days and that he would miss her. A lot. What he didn't tell her was where he was going and why. Rachel didn't ask. She felt it would sound possessive of her after the deep intimacy they had shared in her trailer, as though she now had some claim on him that entitled her to keep track of him. Privately, though, she was a little hurt by his failure to confide in her. She was also scared by his mysterious absence, and she didn't know why.

She was being silly, of course. He said he would be back. There was no reason to suppose he wouldn't return, that his abrupt departure had anything to do with what had happened in the trailer. She refused to believe that their lovemaking had ultimately alarmed him, that he was bolting because, with his history, he couldn't handle the potential consequences.

But Rachel couldn't shake the hollow loneliness that descended on her when Craig was suddenly no longer there on the lot. She oughtn't to have missed him so much. She was certainly busy enough dealing with problems. Everything seemed to go wrong at once.

The temperamental Karl Dvorak got into a fight with one of the work crew over the care of his tigers. She'd no sooner arbitrated the dispute when the three Ortega brothers came to her with sober faces.

"Rachel," Julio explained, doing his best to suppress his excitement, "we've had an offer from the Ringling outfit. They have an opening on one of their units, and they're inviting us to fill it."

Rachel was distressed. The spectacular quadruple somersault the fliers had added to their act had been a great draw. Apparently, it had also drawn a Ringling talent scout. The brothers didn't want to be disloyal and promised to stay until she located a replacement for them, but she could see they were anxious not to miss this marvelous opportunity. She hated to see them go, but she couldn't hold them back. She had to be happy for them, even though the performance would suffer without them.

The day after the Ortegas made their announcement, Felix roused her out of a sound sleep in the middle of the night. Wrapping herself in a robe, Rachel met him at her trailer door. "What is it, Felix?"

"Better get your bag. It's the bulls."

"Sick? Which one?"

"*All* of them."

Rachel lost no time in joining him. It was a serious situation. The elephants were not only valuable but essential to the show, everyone's favorite performers.

She examined them with care. The poor beasts, with slobbering mouths and slime running out of their trunks, were shaking as though in pain. She conferred with Felix. The elephants were his babies, and he looked worried.

"It looks to me like they ate bad hay," she said.

Felix nodded. "Yeah, that figures. Wayne just told me he wondered a bit about that last delivery, said maybe it didn't look quite right. But then, he figured it was okay since the bulls didn't hesitate over it. We gonna lose any of them, Rachel?"

"Not if I can help it. I'm going to prepare injections of antihistamine. While I'm doing that, I want you and Wayne to mix up a bran-mash gruel. After we get all that into them, we're going to have to see to it that they drink water. Lots of water. We need to clean out their systems."

There was no more sleep for Rachel that night. Along with Felix and Wayne, she sat up with the elephants, forcing them to take quantities of water, checking them periodically.

By midmorning, the bulls were back to normal. Rachel wished she could say the same for herself. She was tired and fighting a splitting headache. She wanted to go back to her trailer and rest. She couldn't. There was too much to be done.

She was alone in the office wagon, struggling through a stack of bills that Molly had laid in front of her, when Craig reappeared. His stalwart, grinning figure climbing into the trailer was a welcome sight.

"You're back!" she said, greeting him in sweet relief.

"Well, sure. Didn't I say I would be?"

She summoned a grateful smile as he leaned over her at the table and kissed her easily on the mouth. He was still grinning as he perched on a corner of the old steel safe, long legs stretched out in front of him. The blue eyes regarding her were lively with an exhilaration she had never seen him generate before. He didn't seem to notice that her eyes were burning with fatigue and a throbbing behind them that didn't want to go away. He was too excited about what he wanted to tell her.

"Miss me?" he teased. "You'd better have."

"You know I did. It—it was a bad three days while you were gone. We had all kinds of difficulties—"

But he didn't want to hear about the troubles she had experienced in his absence. He was eager to explain about his secret errand. "I would have told you where I was going," he said, interrupting her, "but I wanted to be sure it was worthwhile, that I had something solid to bring back to you. Well, now I think I have. I *know* I have."

She wanted to share his boyish enthusiasm. She wanted to properly express her delight in his return. But he had caught her at the worst possible moment. "Craig, do you think we could talk about this when—"

"The Miller and Hodge Circus!" he announced elatedly.

She put down the pen she had been signing checks with. "What?"

"Miller and Hodge," he said. "They're playing now in Indiana. That's where I was."

She stared at him, appalled. "You went to Miller and Hodge? Craig, they're our opposition. Why would you go to them?"

"Because they're highly successful and I wanted to find out what they're doing."

"I know what they're doing." She couldn't prevent the ice from creeping into her voice. "Craig, you don't understand. The Miller and Hodge outfit isn't just the competition. They're—well, there's always been a terrible rivalry between our two circuses. Craig, they did awful things to us. Dad told me about it. They put out rat-sheets against us."

"Rat—*what?*"

"Rat-sheets. Defamatory posters attacking our show. Once, they even started this wild billing war with us. They defaced our posters or covered them with their own. And everybody knows Donelli's has always been what circus people call a Sunday-school show, and proud of it. We've never cheated our customers, but they—"

"Rachel," he said, cutting her off, "when did all this happen? Last year? The year before?"

"Well, no. Mostly it was in my grandfather's day, but—"

"Then don't you think it's time all that was forgotten? I'm sure the Miller and Hodge people have forgotten it long ago."

He made her sound like a fool, as though she were engaged in some ancient blood feud. He didn't understand.

"Look," he said, leaning toward her earnestly, "I don't know what the Miller and Hodge Circus was like in the past, and I don't care to know. What matters is that today they're a clean, profitable operation. So profitable, that they're planning a multi-ring show for next season. There are reasons for that success, Rachel, and I learned what they are."

She had to be fair. She had to listen to his arguments, appreciate them, if she could. She just wished her head would stop hammering so she could think clearly. "All right," she said meekly.

Craig was disappointed. She wasn't reacting the way he had planned. He could feel her already putting up barriers. But, of course, she hadn't heard yet about the things he had seen. Once he told her, she would start to see the possibilities, be as prepared as he was to bring Donelli's into the computer age.

"They have a new big top," he told her, striving to keep a note of conviction in his voice. "Not he usual canvas sections. It's all in one piece. They call it a push-pull tent. It goes up without nearly as much labor and comes down faster. It's weather resistant and a lot stronger and safer."

Rachel already knew about that polyvinyl nightmare he was describing, and she shuddered inwardly at the prospect of such a big top going up on a Donelli stand. But all she said was a quiet, "It—it sounds very expensive."

"I know. It's nothing you could afford this season, but it's something to be kept in mind for the future. The patrons seemed to be fascinated by it. I was."

"What else?" she asked him.

"The performance. That's where it counts. High-tech acts. The crowds over there loved them."

He went on to explain all he had seen. A thrilling high-wire motorcycle. A ponderous mechanical apparatus called the Wheel of Death. Another space-age device known as Captain Astronaut. Even the Miller and Hodge seating was nontraditional, trucks whose sides folded down in tiers.

When he was finished telling her about the modern wonders he had experienced, he asked a hopeful, "Well, what do you think?"

He was proposing that she adopt these things for Donelli's Circus. She knew that's what was on his mind. And she hated them. She hated every one of those plastic marvels.

She didn't answer him for a moment. She rubbed her fingers against her temples. The headache was very bad now. She wished she could be as delighted as he was by what he had seen. Maybe if he hadn't come to her with all this when everything seemed to be going wrong at once, then— No! How could she ever be receptive to such changes when they went against everything she believed a circus should be?

"Rachel?"

"I think," she said slowly, honestly, "that they sound like a slick special-effects movie, not a circus."

She was rejecting his ideas. He had come to her proudly and happily with his bag of solutions, laying them at her feet like a hard-won trophy, and she was kicking them away. It hurt. It felt as though she was rejecting him.

He tried not to take it personally, to be reasonable about it. He tried to reach her with logical persuasion, but he was suddenly not feeling very patient about it. "Rachel, you have a good show here. A damn good show. But it's not enough. No operation can thrive without growth and expansion. It's the name of the game."

She shook her head obstinately. "Not that way. Not with a lot of technical wizardry that would destroy everything Donelli's has come to stand for. Craig, I grew up on this circus. I heard all the stories of what my people went through since my great-grandfather came from Italy to start the first Donelli's. The harsh conditions of trouping with a little wagon show, the toughness and courage that was needed to keep it going. But *never*, no matter how bad the times were, did they fail to preserve the grassroots traditions of a pure circus program. I tried to tell you about those traditions that day at Baraboo, how unique and precious they are. Now you're asking me to sacrifice them. If I did that, we wouldn't be Donelli's."

"Wrong," he said, unable to help his anger now, "you'd just be nothing at all, because you'll cease to exist. Is that what you want?"

"That's not fair!" she cried. "I am willing to update the show, but not if it means compromising our standards."

"No," he said, "you aren't willing to change at all, Rachel. That's the whole problem. You're stubbornly keeping Donelli's in the cave age." He got to his feet, confronting her with his chilling gaze. "But the bottom line here is you won't trust me, and that being the case..."

She stared at him, trying to ignore the pain stabbing through her head. She was beginning to understand why his sudden departure three days ago had scared her. She was scared now. "What—what are you telling me?"

What was he trying to say? he wondered. That the situation was impossible? Yeah, that was about it. She wasn't going to let him fight for her, and he could no longer stand the frustration of her resistance.

Rachel had taught him how to care again, how to be close to her family. On that level, she had offered him something vital, something he'd been grateful for, but now, she refused to let him matter where it really counted. And what she had already given him was falling apart on him, because if she had no confidence in his judgment, if she wouldn't let him help her, then the rest didn't mean anything.

What was he doing here, anyway? Driving stakes, selling soft drinks in the big top, fighting mud and heat. This wasn't his world. He didn't belong. He never had, actually. Wasn't that what she was, in effect, telling him?

He'd made a big mistake. He had let her get next to his heart. Now he was paying for that error with the pain of her repudiation. So what was the point in hanging around and suffering even more when, without her faith in him, they didn't stand a chance? He should have known. He should have remembered that his relationships always had fatal flaws that, sooner or later, made them go wrong. He had an idea that this failed involvement was going to hurt worse than any other and for a long time to come. But if he got out now...

"I guess what I'm telling you, Rachel," he said bitterly, "is that there isn't anything more I can do. You didn't want my earlier recommendations, now you don't want these. There's not much point in my being here then, is there? Not when there are businesses back in St. Louis that I *can* help."

She gazed at him, stricken. "You—you're leaving?"

One of his tawny eyebrows lifted in a self-mockery meant to hide his anguish. "Let's just say that, in your language, I'm blowing the show."

What about us? she wanted to cry out to him. But he was gone from the trailer before she could say anything. Or maybe her pride wouldn't let her plead those words. That, and her blinding headache.

Felix didn't have to knock on the motel room door. It already stood wide open. He didn't wait for any invitation. He went on in. The first thing he noticed was the pair of suitcases sitting on the floor, ready to be loaded into the trunk of the car out front. That was a bad sign. Even more damning was the sight of Hollister coming out of the bathroom where he had been packing his shaving kit. He was wearing his most severe business suit. He hadn't been dressed like that in days.

Felix took the cigar out of the corner of his mouth and tucked it into his shirt pocket. Though he rarely smoked them anymore, he did save them to chew on out of habit. "So," he sniffed, "it's true. You are pulling out."

Craig eyed him with a caustic smile as he leaned over to add the shaving kit to the rest of his luggage. "Somebody been complaining about that?" he wondered dryly.

The older man frowned at him. "If you mean Rachel, she ain't said a word. But we're not fools. We can put two and two together. Lucille saw you storming away from the office wagon, and Molly caught Rachel looking like a funeral."

Craig straightened and faced him. "And you lost no time in rushing over here to verify it. Well, don't worry, Felix. This time, I won't be back. I'm off your backs for good. That ought to be cause for a real celebration in the cookhouse tent."

He turned away to look for his car keys on the dresser. Felix didn't say anything for a moment, and then he growled an angry, "You got some nerve, Hollister."

Craig halted, staring at him in speechless surprise.

"All right," Felix said, "so we didn't want you in the beginning. But all that changed, didn't it, when you got to be one of us? Sure, you got to be real close, part of the family. And now you want to desert us just when we come to care and count on you."

"You're crazy! The only reason any of you accepted me was for Rachel's sake. I can see that now."

"Yeah? Then why am I so damn mad? Okay, so we care because of Rachel. We don't want Rachel to be hurt. But, hell, it isn't just her we got to watch out for. Now we've got *you* to worry about, too. Why do you think I come over here like this? Come on, what's this all about? Just what happened between the two of you that's got you hightailing it back to St. Louis?''

Craig was touched by the older man's gruff expression of affection, but he was still mistrustful. He had spent a lifetime running away from such offered sentiments, and he supposed he was about to run away from this one. He couldn't help it. The disappointments in his life had been too frequent and too harsh. But maybe he did owe Felix an explanation. That much he could return, anyway.

"All right," he said. "The truth, plain and simple, is that I wanted to do something for Rachel and her circus. I started out helping her and ended up realizing that she didn't want my help. Fact is, none of you really wanted my help, ever.''

Felix surprised him again after he had finished explaining all that had happened in the office wagon. He didn't side with Rachel. He didn't offer a single argument in her favor. All he did was thank Craig, shake his hand and solemnly leave the motel.

Felix knew just where to look for Rachel. As a child, whenever she had been desperately unhappy and wanted to be alone with her thoughts, when even Napoleon's company wouldn't do, she had hid out in the big top. While she was still very little, she had crawled under the seats. Later, when she had gotten too big for that, she had climbed into the top level of the bleachers. It was still her favorite refuge in times of despair.

That's exactly where Felix found her when he returned from the motel, high up in the gloom of the deserted big top, looking lost and lonely. He mounted the bleachers and settled down beside her.

Rachel, chin in hands, turned to look at him. She wasn't eager for his company, even though her head was no longer tormenting her. A couple of aspirin had taken care of the pain. But nothing could help the ache in her heart.

"Did you need me for something?" she asked.

"Not until this afternoon's performance."

"What is it, then?"

"I just got back from saying goodbye to Craig Hollister."

She hesitated, then nodded slowly. "I see."

He shook his head. "Afraid you don't, Rachel."

She dropped her elbows from her knees and sat up straight. "What's that supposed to mean?"

"Hollister told me what happened." Felix removed the fedora from his head and turned it slowly by the brim. "I don't know that he isn't right, Rachel. I don't know that maybe it isn't time to bring some of the changes to Donelli's that he's asking for."

Rachel stared at him in astonishment. "Felix, *you,* of all people! You've hated the idea of losing the traditional circus more than anyone else on the show!"

"Yeah, well, maybe I was wrong. I been thinkin' about it...." He paused and scratched at his balding head. "The thing is, Rachel, I believe your daddy would have approved of the idea. I believe he would have said that, if that's the way for Donelli's to survive, then we got to go for it. We got to bring the show out of mothballs. Doesn't mean we have to lose the traditions that count. All it means is we blend the new with the old, get us a fresh Donelli's. I think that's all Craig is asking for. The guy cares, Rachel. He cares about us, and he cares about you."

"If he cares so much, then why did he walk out like that?"

Felix's shoulders lifted in a small shrug. "The man's got pride, Rachel, and it's hurting now. Same as yours."

She didn't answer him. She gazed off into the murky twilight of the tent.

Felix laid a comforting hand on her knee. "Don't make sense that the two of you are at odds like this. Not when you belong together. Everybody on the lot knows that." He clapped his hat back on his head and got to his feet. "Think about it, Rachel."

She did think about it after Felix left her. In fact, in the next couple of days, that's all she *could* think about. There were a lot of uncertainties in her churning thoughts, but one thing was absolutely clear. She was in love with Craig Hollister. If she'd had any doubts on the subject before this, then they had all evaporated. She was in love with him, and she was miserable without him.

When she confided this realization to Felix after thanking him for his lecture to her in the big top, he challenged her with a brusque, "Yeah? So, what do you intend to do about it?"

Rachel had already decided exactly what she was going to do. She was going to put the circus in the capable hands of Felix and Ray for a few days and fly to St. Louis. She would go to Craig and tell him how wrong she had been, that she was ready to work with him to change Donelli's, to modernize the whole operation along the lines he had recommended, just as soon as funds permitted it.

She wasn't sure how Craig felt about her now, whether he reciprocated her love. But they would discuss that, too, including her lingering concern over his feelings for his late wife. Surely, they would talk it all out, and maybe... But she wouldn't go any further than that. Not until she had seen him. Not until she was in his arms again.

Rachel was in a state of euphoria when she went into the ring that night for her riding act. A seat was waiting for her on a plane out of Milwaukee tomorrow afternoon. She couldn't know then that there would be a sad irony about her need for that flight to St. Louis.

The big top was packed that evening with a crowd that seemed to be enjoying every exciting minute of the show.

Rachel considered it a good omen. They were three-quarters through the program when the local sheriff arrived on the lot. He spoke to Rachel and Felix in grave tones outside the back door.

"Hate to interrupt your show like this, folks, but we just got a weather warning. A bad storm is expected within the next hour with severe winds, and with that crowd in your tent..."

Rachel and Felix assured the sheriff that they knew exactly what had to be done. It was a situation all circus troupers dreaded but which they were prepared to handle. Ray was beckoned from the ring and the circumstances explained to him. The ringmaster went back to his mike just as Lucille completed her poodle act.

Panic in the audience had to be avoided at all costs. He explained to them calmly why the performance had to be cut short and how they were to safely evacuate the tent.

The welfare of the patrons was always the first consideration. Nothing could be done about safeguarding the circus itself until the last spectator had been cleared from the big top and conducted to his car. By then, the wind was rising threateningly with lightning forking across the inky western sky.

The backyard was a sea of urgent activity as every man and woman on the show hurried to secure the animals and equipment. The other tents on the lot had already been lowered and packed away in preparation for the next haul, but the big top was in danger.

"No time to get it down!" Felix shouted over the commotion. "All we can do now is fight to save it!"

None of them needed to be told how vital the big top was, or how every effort had to be made to prevent its destruction. As the first savage winds tore through the long rural valley where they were pitched, briefly showering hailstones the size of acorns, their frantic cries ripped through the air.

"Lash those jumper cables good and tight! If the quarter poles go and lift out of their sockets, they'll shred the canvas like threshers!"

"Seal the doors! Any wind gets under the top, she'll go like a sailing ship!"

"Come on, extra stakes on the line! Tie 'em down! We got to keep her in the air!"

For long minutes, while the wind raced across the lot with ever-increasing violence, bringing sheets of stinging rain behind it, the crew battled feverishly, valiantly, to save the big top. But even as they struggled to hold down the billowing, whipping fabric against the onslaught of gusts mounting now to a gale velocity, there came the horrible sound of rending canvas as first one seam and then another parted above them.

"We're losing her! Oh, damn it all, we're losing her!"

With the wind having forced its way into the big top, there was no saving it. Fall lines snapped under the strain, poles cracked, stakes were picked up and hurled. With a wild ripping and tearing of canvas, with the bellowing of wind and thunder and men's curses, the big top exploded like a bomb, collapsing across the muddy lot in worthless tatters.

They gathered with somber faces in the resurrected cookhouse tent early the next morning to assess their situation. Rachel was thankful that there had been no injuries and that all of the equipment, including the seating, was still intact. But the big top had been reduced to an irreparable debris, and there was no insurance to cover a disaster of this magnitude. The premiums for wind damage to circus canvas were simply not affordable for small shows like Donelli's.

Rachel was proud of her family. They were circus troupers, and they would not accept defeat.

"So we had a blowdown," the tiny, spirited Buster said. "We're not going to let that finish us, are we?"

He was expressing the courage and determination that all of them were feeling.

"No," Rachel agreed, knowing that if she had their support in this emergency, she would make every effort not to fail them. "We won't quit. If there's a way to go on playing our route, we'll do it. Felix?"

He nodded and cleared his throat. "Yeah. Well, it's all arranged. I got through to our next stand. There's an arena there, and we can have it, so we go indoors to play that one. There's even a good chance that we'll get an auditorium for the engagement after that, but for the following dates..."

"I know," Rachel said solemnly. "It means that if we're to finish the season, we have no choice but to come up with a replacement canvas. I'm flying to St. Louis this afternoon." Not for the reason she had so eagerly anticipated twelve hours ago, she thought forlornly.

"I'm going to see Mr. Sutherland at the bank," she went on. "I hope to convince him to lend us the price of another big top."

"And if he says no?" Lucille asked anxiously.

"Let's not even think about it," Ray said.

Molly took Rachel aside after the meeting, wanting to know, "What happens to your riding act while you're gone?"

"It gets omitted from the program, I'm afraid."

Molly stubbornly shook her blond head. "That's no good, Rachel. You know it's a favorite with audiences, and with our situation being what it is now, it's important to show people that our performances aren't going to suffer in any way. I just don't think you should leave that hole in the program."

"Molly, you're not suggesting..."

The older woman's small mouth puckered into an indignant pout. "You seem to be forgetting who taught you that Pete Jenkins routine in the first place and that I used to

perform a popular version of it on this same show for a
good many seasons, as well as work the liberty horses.''

Rachel didn't want to offend the woman by pointing out
that she hadn't entered the ring in years. ''Molly, I don't
know. Have you talked this over with Felix?''

''Yes, and Ray, too. They're willing, if you agree to it and
providing I look all right in a practice session. And I will.
I'm not that past it.''

Rachel was reluctant. She didn't think it was a good idea,
but Molly was insistent. She surrendered in the end. The
bank was waiting for her.

The bank president's office had thick carpeting on the
floor and tasteful prints on its paneled walls. The windows
framed an imposing view of the St. Louis skyline with its
famous arch. But Rachel was scarcely aware of her sur-
roundings as she sat in a deep leather chair and nervously
faced Hank Sutherland across his massive mahogany desk.
She had come directly from the airport to plead her case.
Since Donelli's Circus was based in Missouri, there had been
a mention on the St. Louis news about the loss of the big top
in Wisconsin. The banker had caught the item, but Rachel
provided him with full details before making her earnest request.

Now she waited tensely for his judgment. The suspense
was awful as she watched his face, hoping to catch some sign
of approval in his expression. But his face remained carefully impassive. Only the long silence told her anything, and
she found it discouraging.

Finally, as he slowly fingered his reddish moustache, he
answered her with deep regret. ''Rachel, I'm sorry. I'm very
sorry, but I can't give you the funds you need. If it were up
to me personally, I wouldn't hesitate. You know how I've
always felt about Donelli's. But I'm responsible to our officers and a board of directors. There are people here who
are already unhappy because I've carried you to this extent.

They think it's a bad investment we need to get out from under. And now if I were to go and authorize a further loan— Well, you can see why I don't dare.''

Rachel's heart sank. She could hardly speak for her disappointment and depression. "What—what happens next, then? Where do we go from here?''

He gazed at her unhappily. "I hate to say it, Rachel, but unless a miracle comes along, you'd better prepare yourself and your people for the last of Donelli's. Of course, we will honor the agreement to carry you the rest of this season. Providing, that is, you can arrange enough indoor dates, but after that . . .'' He spread his hands in a gesture of inevitability.

Rachel smiled bitterly. "A miracle? I'm afraid Donelli's has been in short supply of those lately.'' There was no hope then, nowhere else to turn. With the circus's credit already at rock bottom, another bank would be useless. She felt sick and helpless.

She thought of Craig. She couldn't help thinking about him, wondering if he was somewhere nearby. She wanted to go to him, feel his arms around her. But a terrible suspicion had crept into her thoughts. She couldn't resist asking the banker, "Mr. Sutherland, did—did Craig Hollister report back to you?''

Was it her imagination, or did the banker suddenly look wary? "Yes, he's back.''

"And did he turn in his last recommendation for Donelli's?''

She suddenly regretted asking the question. She didn't want to know. She didn't want to believe that anything Craig might have said in his final analysis could have determined Hank Sutherland's negative decision just now. Craig wouldn't betray her family like that. He *couldn't*. How could she even let herself suspect it?

Before her devastating fear could be confirmed or denied, the banker's assistant interrupted them, marching in from her outside office. "Sorry to intrude," she said, "but there's an urgent call for Ms. Donelli." She turned to Rachel. "You can take it on the private line in the reception area if you'd like."

Rachel excused herself and followed the woman from the room, not daring to guess who this call was from or what it could be about. But she was trembling when she picked up the phone and identified herself.

"Rachel," the familiar voice of her ringmaster answered back, "it's Ray. I—I hate to have to tell you this, but Molly took a fall."

Rachel's heart leaped into her throat. "What happened?"

"She missed a trick at this afternoon's performance. She went down under Warrior's hooves, and before she could roll out, he kicked her in the head. Felix and Lucille are with her now at the hospital. Rachel, it's—it's not good. She's in a coma, and they don't know yet what her chances are."

Rachel shut her eyes, shaken by the news. Oh, dear God, not another tragedy! Not Molly! How much more suffering could her poor circus family take?

"Rachel?"

Recovering from the blow, she managed to speak calmly to the ringmaster. "Ray, I'm leaving right away. I'll catch the first flight back. Tell Felix I'm coming."

Nine

Craig was not in the bank when Rachel hurried through its doors. Nor was he even in St. Louis. At that moment, he was standing in the office wagon of the Miller and Hodge Circus, now playing central Illinois.

Like Hank Sutherland, Craig had heard on the early-morning news of the blowdown in Wisconsin and the total loss of the Donelli big top. He had realized that Rachel's show was finished unless she somehow acquired another canvas. He had also understood, better than anyone, how unlikely that prospect was.

He hadn't hesitated. He had phoned the bank, told them he wouldn't be in that day, checked on the current where-abouts of the Miller and Hodge outfit and headed across the river in his car.

It was an impulsive act, but what else could he do? Rachel had entrusted her two most valuable assets to him—her circus family and her heart. He couldn't forget that. He couldn't fail her now when she needed him so desperately, when there was no one else to turn to. He had no illusions about the bank giving her more money. So he had to help her himself, whatever their hopeless differences.

He was a fool about her, of course. Speeding across the Illinois flatlands, he had told himself that he ought to be making every effort to get over her. Instead, he was about to get involved again in her affairs.

He had missed her from the moment he had walked out of her office wagon, his treacherous body aching for her. That ache hadn't lessened in the past couple of days. If anything, it had intensified, making him remember in the long, torturous nights their wild, sweet lovemaking in her trailer. But he was going to continue to resist the blatant yearning of his body. No matter how good they were in bed together, it wasn't enough when their attitudes about the circus were in such opposition. Anyway, with his history, Rachel was better off without him. He had no business getting intimate with any decent woman. Not when he couldn't ultimately handle it, not when there wasn't the solution she deserved. He was going to help her, all right, hopefully without her knowledge, but he wasn't going to try to see her again.

Now, facing Al Miller, the burly owner of the Miller and Hodge Circus, Craig told himself all over again that he was being a sentimental fool about her blasted circus. But his self-anger didn't stop him from earnestly explaining to the other man what he wanted.

"I remember your mentioning to me during my visit, when we discussed your new tent, that you still have your old big top from last season."

Miller nodded. "That's right. We got it in storage over at our winter quarters in Indiana. Still in good shape, too. Why are you interested?"

"I want to buy it from you."

"But that's our backup canvas! That's why we kept it, in case of an emergency. Anyhow," he asked suspiciously, "why would *you* want to acquire a circus big top?"

"It isn't for me," Craig told him honestly. "It's for the Donelli show."

Miller understood. "Oh, jeez, yeah, I heard about their loss. It's tough when that happens, but why should I do the opposition the favor of turning over my canvas to them?"

"Because they badly need it and you don't. You told me yourself that your new big top is completely weatherproof, that it will last for years. You'll never use that backup canvas. You might as well make a sale on it. I'll pay you a good price."

The circus man looked suspicious again. "The Donelli people send you down here?"

"No, I'm doing this on my own."

"Wouldn't care to tell me why that is, would you?"

"Not particularly."

"Uh-huh." Miller drummed his thick fingers on the desktop, considering the proposition while Craig waited tautly for his decision. "Oh, what the hell, why not? Circus troupers in trouble should help each other, so we'll let bygones be bygones."

Craig smiled in relief. They discussed price and agreed on a fair amount. Craig could easily afford it. There was a large sum of money in one of his accounts that, until now, he hadn't been able to bring himself to touch. But he didn't tell Miller that. He had never discussed that money with anyone, preferring to bury the unhappy associations of its existence. But now, some of it was needed.

"One thing," Craig insisted as he produced his checkbook. "I don't want the Donelli outfit knowing who bought this canvas for them. Let them think you're donating it as a gesture of goodwill." He didn't want Rachel feeling obligated to him. Anyway, he wasn't sure she would accept the big top if she learned he was paying for it. Why risk another painful complication?

"Whatever you say," Miller agreed. "You want to play silent benefactor, that's your business. I'll call winter quarters and have them truck the canvas up to Donelli's stand first thing."

While Craig wrote out the check, Miller leaned back in his chair, remarking casually, "Guess the Donelli show *is* due for a break. They sure seem haunted by disasters lately. First the blowdown, now this accident on top of it."

Craig gazed at him sharply. "What accident?"

"You don't know?"

"I've come from St. Louis, not Wisconsin. What accident?" he demanded again.

"Woman took a bad fall in the ring."

"What woman? What did you hear?"

"Well, hey, I'm real sorry, but I never guessed you didn't—"

"Never mind that! Just tell me!"

"One of the girls on our show passed it on. See, the cat trainer over at Donelli's was sweet on her when he was with us last season. He talked to her on the phone just a bit ago. Said things were a mess on Donelli's and wished he was back here. That's when he mentioned they'd been playing an auditorium this afternoon and that the woman doing the Pete Jenkins routine went down under her horse. Pretty bad, I guess. On the critical list. They're not sure if she'll make it."

Craig went rigid with shock and fear. "Pete Jenkins? Are you *sure* it was the Pete Jenkins routine?"

"Yeah, she was real clear about that."

Rachel! Oh, dear lord, Rachel! He had to go to her! He had to be with her!

Sick with dread, Craig shoved the check at Miller, stuffed the bill of sale into his pocket and fled the office wagon. Minutes later, he was on the highway, speeding north toward the Wisconsin border.

There was no thought in his head of his recent promise to himself not to see her again. There was only his wild need to reach her, his frantic prayer for her well-being. But under his urgency was a memory tormenting him with pain as sharp as talons. He had lost his wife, he had lost his son. He could never bear another loss like that. He could never survive the despair of losing Rachel. She was the most important being in his life. Without her existence, nothing would ever matter again. Why hadn't he realized that? Why had it taken this hellish accident to make him understand? His sweet, beautiful Rachel!

His?

And then it struck him. She did belong to him. She *was* his. He loved her. He had been in love with her for weeks now. He had known he was in love with her when he walked out on her. It was probably the real reason he had left. He had simply been too scared to handle it, to even admit to himself what he felt. And now he was terrified because he might lose what he had just found.

He thought about stopping somewhere and trying to phone someone who could tell him what he was desperate to know. But he didn't want to waste time struggling to put a call through to the circus. He just wanted to reach Rachel. He went on driving.

Mercifully, the traffic was light, but it was well after dark before Craig reached the town where Donelli's was playing. The route sheet still in his possession had told him where to go, but he didn't know where the show was pitched. Before he could stop to ask, he noticed signs directing motorists to the local trauma center. He followed the signs, realizing that Rachel must have been taken to the nearest hospital.

He found the building, parked the car and rushed inside, his heart in his throat. There was a young woman on duty in the reception area. She was busy on the phone. He leaned over the counter, interrupting her conversation with an insistent, "The woman from the circus who was injured! Is she here?"

Distracted, the receptionist pointed to a corridor on the left, and said hastily, "You'll find her people in the waiting room at the far end. They'll fill you in." Handing him a visitor's pass, she went back to her call.

There was a late-night silence in the deserted corridor as Craig strode swiftly along its length, his heart still racing with apprehension. Straight ahead of him, framed in the open doorway of the waiting room, two familiar figures huddled side by side on a sofa. The presence of Felix and Lucille confirmed his fear.

Until now, Craig had hoped that it might all be a mistake, even that Rachel's injury hadn't been severe. But Felix looked haggard with worry as he hunched forward, hands dangling helplessly between his parted legs. Lucille, squeezed beside him, had a comforting hand on his arm.

Sensing Craig's presence as he moved into the room, they looked up at him with startled surprise. None of them spoke. They just stared at one another for a long moment.

And then a soft, husky voice behind Craig whispered a disbelieving, "Craig?"

He whirled so suddenly and so swiftly that Rachel almost lost control of the paper cups in her hands. She'd been in the adjoining refreshment area getting coffee from the machine for Lucille and Felix. Now, face-to-face with Craig, she was having trouble realizing that he was actually here. He was gazing at her with the same disbelief on his face. He didn't speak; he just looked.

"Craig?" she prompted him again.

Something seemed to snap in him then. With a hoarse groan, he closed the distance between them in two quick strides. Rachel was snatched against him, the coffee sent flying from her hands. She felt herself being crushed in his arms, held so fiercely that she couldn't breathe. She didn't understand it, but she welcomed it.

It was with reluctance that he finally released her. He held her away in order to look down into her face, needing to assure himself that she was all right.

Rachel stared at him, shocked. There were tears in his eyes! There were *actual* tears of relief in his eyes! He looked terrible. His face was drawn, shadowed with the stubble of a beard, his hair and clothes mussed. He also looked potently, wonderfully male.

One of her hands, free now of the coffee cups, which were somewhere on the floor, came up to wipe at the tears on his face. Something squeezed around her heart at the feel of that wetness, something poignant and beautifully moving.

"Are—are you okay?" she managed to ask him.

He caught her hand, pressing it to his cheek. "Yeah," he said, his voice gritty with emotion. "Yeah, I'm fine. I thought you were injured. They said the woman who did the Pete Jenkins routine was badly injured."

"It's Molly, Craig. She was filling in for me. It's Molly who was hurt."

He turned his head, glancing sympathetically at Felix. Felix and Lucille were still on the sofa, gazing at him in bewilderment. "Molly?" he asked blankly.

Rachel explained how the other woman had come to replace her in the ring. She started to ask him how he had heard of the accident, but he interrupted. "How is she?"

Lucille answered the question for him in a somber voice. Felix was too distraught over his wife to say anything. "They have her in intensive care. She's been in a coma since the accident."

"A CAT scan determined there's a blood clot," Rachel added. "A specialist came out from Milwaukee. He's going to operate. They're preparing her now for surgery. All we can do is wait."

Craig joined them in their long vigil. He had thought that nothing else could matter as long as Rachel was safe. But he was wrong. Molly mattered. She mattered a great deal. That was when he realized how much these people had come to mean to him. There was no doubt about it anymore. He was as bonded now to the circus family as Rachel. They were his family, too, his responsibility, his beloved concern. In a better moment, he would share their joy. In this moment, he shared their tense prayers for Molly's recovery. He didn't question it. He just believed in it. It felt right. It felt good.

Their differences forgotten in the face of Molly's ordeal, Rachel and Craig sat side by side on another sofa. He held her hand, listened to her express her guilt about Molly and assured her, along with Lucille and Felix, that she had nothing to reproach herself for. She dozed on his shoulder, and he liked having her there.

Other members of the show came by to hear the latest. Without comment, they accepted Craig's presence in the waiting room. He was one of them. He belonged. They went away again after being promised that the circus would be contacted as soon as there was anything definite to report. Ray was standing by on the show grounds to pass the information.

The doctor stopped in to let them know that Molly was out of surgery. He was cautious about her prognosis, but hopeful. She was still unconscious.

Rachel slept again on Craig's shoulder. He guessed he must have drifted off himself, for the next thing he knew, daylight was streaming through the window and a nurse was there telling Felix that he could see his wife for a few minutes. Felix came back from the visit beaming. Molly had been briefly awake and had recognized him. It looked like she was going to be okay.

They laughed and embraced one another in relief. Then Rachel went to the phone and, after a small delay, managed to get Ray on the line. When she informed the ringmaster that Molly was expected to fully recover, he expressed his gladness and then added a cheerful, "Things are really beginning to look up!"

There was a note of excitement in his voice that puzzled her slightly, but she didn't question it. She went back to the room where the others were waiting.

"Now that Molly's out of danger," she told them, "I'd better get back to the show grounds. We still have two performances to play here."

Lucille said she would remain at the hospital with Felix, but both of them promised to arrive on the lot in time for the afternoon show. They knew Molly would want it that way.

Craig said he would drive Rachel back to the grounds. She welcomed his offer. She didn't know how long he planned to stay in town and was afraid to ask him. But she would take as much of him as she could get for as long as she could get.

Craig had no intention of going back to St. Louis. Not, anyway, until he found the right moment to tell her he loved her. Not before he learned exactly what she felt for him.

He was nervous with her in the car, looking for the opportunity to express his anxious feelings. She was nervous, too. She told him in a halting voice, "Craig, I—I want you to know how wrong I was about your ideas for Donelli's. I realized that after you left."

What had changed her mind? he wondered. Merely her concern for the circus, or was it because she cared as much about him as he cared about her? He didn't know. But her confession gave him new hope.

"So if you're still willing to work with me," she went on, "I am ready to modernize the show. Providing, there *is* a Donelli's after we run out of auditoriums to play."

He assured her he was willing to help her. He didn't tell her about the big top. He wanted her to be surprised.

Rachel didn't disappoint him when, seconds later, they arrived on the lot and she discovered the new big top swelling in the field behind the arena. Her stunned reaction delighted him.

"I—I don't understand," she stammered, climbing from the car. "How did it get here? Where did it come from?"

Ray was there to explain. "Miller and Hodge delivered it. It's their last season's canvas. They heard about our blow-down and wanted to help out. It's a beauty, isn't it?"

Rachel was touched by the gesture and willing to believe that in a crisis, circus troupers were prepared to forget their differences. It was the tradition she had been raised on. Craig said nothing. It was time she was allowed to bury the old vendetta with the Miller and Hodge outfit.

He and Rachel joined the rest of the company in the cookhouse tent where Craig was greeted warmly. Over breakfast, they celebrated Molly's recovery and the new big top that meant the show could go on playing its full route. Craig was still searching for that right moment to talk to her. Rachel offered it to him after they had eaten.

"I feel grubby," she complained. "I need a shower and a change."

"Me, too," he said. "The shower part, anyway. I came away without any extra clothes."

"You can use the bathroom in my trailer," she suggested. "Unless you'd prefer to find a motel." She prayed he didn't.

He did not prefer to find a motel. This was his chance to be alone with her.

When they reached her trailer, she invited him to use the shower first.

He grinned at her wickedly. "What's wrong with using it together?"

Her cheeks went pleasurably hot over the suggestion, but she covered it with a light, "Tempting, but I guess you've never been inside the shower stall of a small trailer. We'd never fit."

"We could try."

She laughed. "Never mind. I'll go first."

He didn't object. He used the opportunity to silently rehearse exactly what he wanted her to know as he slowly paced the cramped area. He still hadn't formed in his mind the words he needed to use when she emerged from the bathroom minutes later in a light robe, her freshly shampooed hair wrapped in a towel.

"There's clean towels on the stool," she said, "and I left you a spare toothbrush on the sink."

Craig decided as he stepped under the shower that there was no way he could plan what he had to tell her. The words would come with the moment. He meant that moment to be very soon.

Rachel was perched on the edge of her bed just off the bathroom when he slipped into the narrow hallway after his shower, a towel slung low around his hips. He meant to ask her if he could borrow a razor to shave off his day-old growth of whiskers. He never made the request.

He was captivated by the sight of her. Her head was tilted far forward as she worked on her thick mane of hair with blow dryer and brush. The tumbled masses caught the light, caressing the lustrous amber tones in the long tresses. The white robe was parted, disclosing her shapely bare legs and a seductive glimpse of her sleek thighs. The deep V of the robe below her throat revealed the equally teasing shadow between her breasts. Craig stood there and stared, actually trembling over the pleasure of watching her.

Rachel finally felt his presence. Laying the blow dryer and the brush on the bed, she lifted her head, sweeping the hair back from her face. The sight of him took her breath away. He was wearing nothing but the towel caught around his lean hips, and he looked powerfully, primitively masculine. He hadn't thoroughly dried himself. Damp spikes of blond hair were plastered attractively against his forehead. There was a dampness, too, in the wedge of hair on his chest. And she could see a few droplets of water clinging to the wiry hairs curling around his navel. She experienced a reckless urge to lick them away, to taste his clean, male skin.

They went on gazing at each other in a silence thick with meaning. His eyes, hot and needful, summoned her. There was no way Rachel could help herself from going to him. She was under a spell. The earthy, primal spell of a man calling to his mate. She stood and walked toward him slowly, the folds of her robe swaying with her hips, whispering against her legs as he waited for her.

The words would have to keep, Craig decided. He couldn't stop himself from having her. He would tell her first with his body what he felt for her.

She came into his arms, and he fitted his body as closely as possible to hers while still permitting her to breathe. Barely. Drawing a ragged breath, Rachel could smell his freshness from the shower, the slick, clean odors of soap and toothpaste and the subtler, musky fragrance that was distinctly his. They made her light-headed. The solid feel of him simply mesmerized her.

He whispered something in her ear, something sexy and explicit in a deep, drowsy huskiness. She answered the first part of his request by lifting her parted mouth to his. Willingly, eagerly. He took her mouth with his, his tongue stroking against hers in a sensual simulation of what he intended to follow.

Rachel whimpered under his sizzling kiss, abandoning herself to the pleasure of feeling the corded muscles of his back beneath her hands clenching his hard flesh. His beard was excitingly rough against her face. She was aware, too, of the brazen evidence of his raging arousal below the towel as his muscled leg inserted itself intimately between hers through the parted robe.

His knee rubbed slowly, tantalizingly back and forth against her thighs. She gasped when he raised the knee and pressed it demandingly against her moist womanhood. The knee stroked against her lovingly, making her so weak with its enticing movements that she would have sagged to the floor if he hadn't been supporting her.

Craig couldn't control the animal sounds low in his throat at his discovery of her nakedness under the robe. "You like that?" he growled in her ear.

"Yes," she whispered. "Yes, I like that very much."

He wanted more of her. He wanted to cherish her whole body. He leaned back against the wall, bearing her weight against his in order to free his hands. Then he burrowed inside the robe above her waist, fondling the silken smoothness of her flesh over her rib cage, finding rapture in the heavy fullness of her breasts. He lowered his head, burying his face in her lushness, taking her turgid nipples deep into his mouth. She moaned, her fingers clutching at his shoulders.

The heat of her inflamed him. He wanted to feel something else down in that satin place where his knee still rested. He wanted to answer the throbbing under his towel.

The trailer was so compact, so small that, without leaving her, he could reach through the doorway of the bathroom. His groping hand found the shelf just inside where he had placed the contents of his pockets. His fingers fumbled in his wallet and withdrew the protection he carried.

Rachel understood his movements. "The bed—"

"No," he said, his voice harsh with need. The bedroom was only steps away, but he wanted her here, just like this.

He slid the robe off her shoulders and dropped it, together with his towel, to the floor. Then, clad in the protection, he braced himself. Hands locked under her alluring bottom, he lifted her over his hard virility and, with one clean thrust, was inside her. The sensation of her tight wetness clasping him was so blindingly satisfying that he swayed drunkenly.

"Craig, it—it feels—"

"I know, sweetheart, I know. Me, too."

"I'm not too heavy for you?"

"No! God, no!"

Her arms and legs were clamped around him. She strained against him, striving to be a part of him. He answered her efforts with his own surging, their flushed bodies celebrating each other in a slow, radiant rhythm.

The rhythm flared and quickened as they sought fulfillment. His release, when it came, was massive, savage, tearing a hoarse cry from his throat. Her own cry matched his as the cataclysm swept through her in a series of powerful convulsions.

The maelstrom had yet to fully subside when Craig, still joined with her, staggered to the bedroom and collapsed with her across the bed.

Drained, they lay there in a mindless euphoria, Rachel's fingers drifting gently through the mat of hair on his chest. After a long moment, Craig reluctantly shifted away from her.

"Don't move," he whispered. "I'll be right back."

He left her briefly to dispose of the protection. Quickly returning, he stretched out beside her again, gathering her into his arms with a happy grunt. He felt lazy and peaceful. Wonderfully peaceful.

"Craig?"

"Mmm?"

"Can—can I ask you something?"

He didn't want to talk. He just wanted to go on cuddling her, maybe leisurely kiss her sultry mouth. He didn't tell her that. "Sure," he said.

His eyes were closed, and he was smiling. She hated to disturb the tender moment, but she had to know. "It's—well, it's about the condoms."

"Huh?"

This was difficult. She tried to find the right words. "You—you never ever take a chance, do you? I mean, even in our most passionate moments, you don't fail to stop and use them properly. You always remember."

His eyes opened and met hers. His gaze was suddenly wary, alert. "People are supposed to be responsible about that kind of thing, Rachel."

"I know, and I appreciate it. I do, but—"

"What?"

"Craig, it's different with you. Every time you've made, well, kind of a big thing out of it. Like it's more than just being careful about the obvious risks."

He moved away from her, levering himself on one elbow. "What are you trying to say, Rachel?"

"I don't know. Just that it seems you're fanatic about preventing a possible pregnancy. That is it, isn't it?"

He didn't answer her. The blue eyes suddenly looked stubborn. She knew he thought her timing was awful, that she had chosen the wrong moment for this discussion. Rachel knew otherwise. After what had just happened between them, realizing how she felt about him and how she hoped he felt about her, the subject couldn't be postponed. She needed to learn just where they were going from here. Or, frightening though the possibility was, not going.

She sat up, hugging herself. "All right," she said quietly, solemnly, "then let me ask you something else. Just how much do I matter to you, Craig? How much do *we* matter?"

She was giving him the opening to tell her what he had been longing all day to put into words, and he suddenly couldn't say it. He was scared. Terrified of where all this was leading.

"Everything," he muttered evasively. "You mean everything to me."

It wasn't good enough. "Exactly what is *everything*, Craig?"

"It means, damn it, that I'm in love with you!" Oh, God, this wasn't the way he had meant to tell her, blurting it out like a hard, angry challenge.

His words should have thrilled her. Why didn't they? "And I love you," she softly confessed.

Her words should have thrilled him. Why didn't they? "That's all that matters then, isn't it?"

She didn't answer him. He searched her face, praying she wouldn't demand what he couldn't give.

Her eyes met his, direct and persistent. "Does this love involve a commitment, Craig?"

"Of course, it does. I want us to live together."

"For how long?"

"What kind of a question is that? For always." *Please be satisfied with that, Rachel,* he pleaded to her silently. *Don't take it where I can't go.*

But she was a woman with traditional values, and he was a fool to hope she might ever settle for less than a traditional commitment.

"Does *always* mean as husband and wife?" she asked him in that same low, earnest voice.

The panic he had been dreading seized him. His palms were sweating, his heart racing as he sat up on the edge of the bed, turning his back so he wouldn't have to meet her eyes.

She waited patiently for his answer. There was no way he could avoid giving her the truth. "No," he said abruptly, hating himself for having to hurt her, hating his weakness.

There was a long silence. He wouldn't look at her. Trembling, Rachel slowly voiced her fearful suspicion. "Craig, are you sure you're in love with me? Are you sure that's what you really feel? Or—or are you still in love with your wife?"

He twisted around on the bed to face her, astonished. There was no hesitation this time in his response. "Is that what you think this is all about? That I can't be married to someone else or have her child because I'm still in love with Lynn?"

"But—isn't it?"

"No! Rachel, I told you that morning Napoleon died that I let Lynn go months ago. Why didn't you believe me?"

"I—I tried, but you seemed so battered about it all that I— Then if that isn't the problem, what is?" She tried to feel relief and couldn't.

He took a deep breath, needing to steady himself. "It's . . . me."

"I don't understand."

"Rachel, I can't handle it. I can't bear the risk of another marriage, another child. I just *can't*. Yesterday, when I thought it was you that I might be losing, I went out of my mind. Don't you see how much worse it would be if you were my wife, if we had children, and something happened? I can't go through that again! I can't be ripped up inside like that!"

"Craig, you can't live with that kind of fear. You can't deny yourself the happiness of marriage and children on the remote chance that—"

"We have a family already," he said desperately, cutting in on her. "We have our family here in the circus. I didn't have that before, and I do now. You gave that to me, and I love you for it. I love you and I want us to be together. Isn't that enough?"

She shook her head sadly. "No, Craig, it isn't. The circus family is important, but it's no substitute for the real thing. I want marriage and children from the man I love, because without them . . ."

She didn't go on. She knew he understood her. But he couldn't answer her. He couldn't give her what she needed. She felt sick inside.

He stared at her silently. There was anguish in his eyes. There was also an unrelenting obstinacy. Miserable, she couldn't bear to go on looking at him.

"I have to go," she said, slipping off the bed on her side. "Ray has two women coming in from the service league that sponsors the circus here. They've volunteered to cover the ticket window and the front door in Molly's absence, but I have to show them what to do before I get ready for the matinee.''

She felt Craig watching her as she reached inside the closet for her clothes and began quickly dressing. He didn't try to stop her. He said nothing as she walked out of the bedroom and left the trailer. Her heart pleaded with him to call out to her, to come after her, not to let her go. But he did nothing.

Ten

From the trailer window, Craig watched Rachel's forlorn figure cross the lot and disappear around the curve of the big top. He had never felt so alone, so helpless. He didn't understand it. How could everything that had been so right suddenly go so wrong? He had no answer for himself.

Turning away from the window, he went into the bathroom and got back into his clothes. He didn't know what to do, where he was supposed to go from here. Life without Rachel was unthinkable, but her ultimatum was unthinkable, as well.

He left the trailer and wandered across the busy circus lot without direction or purpose, feeling like a drifting ship that had lost its anchor.

Felix was back from the hospital. He was at the elephant line talking softly, affectionately to the massive beasts whose waving trunks were never still.

Hands stuffed into his pockets, Craig paused to watch the scene. The older man, sensing his presence, turned around to greet him with a crooked grin.

"I was telling the bulls about Molly," he said. "Bulls is smart. They understand. And they care."

"How is Molly doing?" Craig asked.

"Full of spunk already, or I wouldn't have come away. She'll be back with us in nothing flat." A questing elephant trunk poked over his shoulder. Felix patted it absently as he shrewdly studied Craig's despondent expression. "You look like you could use a friend, Hollister. What's wrong? When you and Rachel left the hospital, you were on cloud nine."

Maybe Felix was right. Maybe what he did badly need in this desolate moment was a friend. But he hesitated. He wasn't used to confiding his private pain.

Felix understood his reluctance. "Hey," he coaxed, "family now, remember?"

Craig smiled at him gratefully. "Yeah, I remember."

"So, okay, let's talk, then."

Before he could object, Craig found himself sitting on a bale of hay with Felix perched on another, listening to him while he shared his despair.

Felix was silent when the situation had been explained. Craig was disappointed. But, then, why should he have expected a miraculous answer to a problem that seemed to have no solution? Anyway, how could the older man relate to a fear he had never personally experienced? But Craig was wrong about that.

Felix took a cigar out of his shirt pocket and started to chew on it slowly. "I guess you'd have no reason to know that Molly's not my first wife."

Craig was surprised. "No, I didn't know that."

"That's right. I was married before. Long time ago. We were just kids. Traveled with a dog-and-pony show. That was before I came with Donelli's. Not much of a circus. Conditions was real rough, and we didn't have an extra dime to spare between us. Certainly nothing to cover a doctor or medical expenses when she got pregnant. Smart-nosed snots that we were, we thought we didn't need any of that when we had a woman on the show claiming to have midwife skills.''

"What happened?'' Craig asked, feeling that he already knew.

"She died in childbirth,'' Felix said flatly. "The baby, too. Chewed me up pretty bad inside. Bad enough that I wasn't ever again going to face anything like that. And for a long time, I didn't. Then Molly came along. She didn't leave me any choice about it. If I wanted her, it was either a wedding ring or nothing. Well, I wanted her, all right. So I shut my eyes and took the plunge. Never been sorry about it, either.'' He rubbed his nose, removed the cigar from his mouth and studied it carefully. "See, Hollister, your situation ain't so unusual.''

Craig stared at him. "How did you handle it? How did you make the decision?''

"Oh, when it come right down to it, it was pretty simple. It just sort of occurred to me that nothing in life that's really worth anything comes without a risk. And Molly was worth plenty.'' He nodded wisely. "Yeah, it was that easy.''

He's right, Craig thought in sudden wonder. It wasn't complicated at all. It was no more involved than one essential question: Which did he fear more, losing Rachel or the risk of marriage and children?

Five minutes ago, he wouldn't have had an answer to that question. He did now. He wanted Rachel, risks and all. Because it was just as Felix said. Nothing worth anything comes without risk.

The relief of his realization filled Craig with joy. He wanted to shout his happiness. He wanted to find Rachel and tell her how wrong he had been. He wanted to hold her in his arms and assure her that he was ready to face anything to preserve their togetherness. And then he caught Felix watching him slyly.

"Never mind," the older man said. "You don't have to tell me. I can see it plain on your face. Easy decision, huh? Now all you have to do is go and tell Rachel you made it."

Craig nodded with forceful determination. "That's right. I'm prepared to convince her that I want her on any terms."

"Good. That's real good. Because at this point, leatherneck, you're gonna have to prove your need for her. Words alone ain't gonna do it. Not now. She's not gonna trust that you just turned around this quick with a complete change of heart. We know it was that simple, because underneath, that's the way you really felt all the time. But Rachel's gonna need something stronger than that to win her. Women are like that, you see."

In his innocence, Craig chuckled dryly. "You think I ought to demonstrate my eagerness for her by carrying her off into the sunset over my saddle?"

Felix was still looking sly. "There's more than one way to be a hero. And a woman does like her man to be a hero for her."

Craig frowned at him. "What are you scheming under that pachyderm hide of yours?"

It was the older man's turn to chuckle. "Maybe just a little circus persuasion. Like, say, meeting her on her own turf inside the big top, where she's vulnerable."

Craig considered him with growing suspicion. "This isn't something I'm going to like, is it?"

Felix shrugged, challenging him with a casual, "I don't know. You afraid of sacrificing that precious dignity of yours to show her just how much you care?"

"Yeah. How?"

"I was kinda thinkin' of you making an unscheduled appearance in the ring this afternoon during her Pete Jenkins routine."

"No! That's crazy!"

"Don't think so. You know what they say, Hollister, actions speak louder than words. 'Course, if you don't love her enough to risk a little harmless foolery to get her..."

"Stop it, Felix. I'm not going into the ring. What would I do in the ring?"

"What were you doing driving tent stakes, helping to raise the canvas, being a candy butcher? If memory serves me, you've done just about a bit of everything on this circus. Except, uh, maybe playing a clown."

Craig exploded. "*Clown?* Me go into that circus ring in a clown getup and— Ohh, no!"

"Sure, why not? You could do it. We could show you just what to do. That would get to Rachel like nothing else could. The power of humor, Hollister. The power of humor." Felix grinned wickedly. "Besides which, it ought to be a helluva lot of fun."

"Yeah, for you, not me. Forget it. No way. Absolutely not. Uh-uh."

What am I doing here? Craig asked himself in a mounting panic as he sat miserably on a prop trunk in the end of the big wardrobe van known as clown alley. *How did I let myself get talked into this? I must be out of my mind. I have to be out of my mind.*

He was surrounded by them, cut off from any possible escape. Felix had rounded up every one of the circus's clowns, including a husband-and-wife team. They stood in front of him, at his sides and behind him. There were only six of them, counting Felix, but they felt like an army.

For the past five minutes, they had been watching silently while Buster, Donelli's head clown, perched on a high stool in front of Craig and studied him intently from every angle. No conspiracy had ever been organized with more dedicated earnestness.

Craig, growing unhappier by the second as six pairs of eyes bored into him, could take it no longer. "Uh, look," he said, breaking the taut silence, "this is a big mistake. It's not going to work. I could never bring it off."

They ignored his objections. He endured another agonizing moment of scrutiny, then cleared his throat again. "Yeah, let's just forget it. Rachel would never go for it, anyway. I mean, I appreciate what you're trying to do and all, but it's nuts to think I could ever pass as a clown. I'll find another way. Okay?"

He started to rise from the trunk, reaching for the white towel they had looped around his neck. Gloria, professionally known as Moonbeam, slapped his hand away and shoved him back. "Shh," she hissed at him. "Buster is about to have one of his inspirations."

Oh, fine, Craig thought with a helpless groan as he settled back on the trunk. Just great. I'm no better than a guinea pig. A dumb guinea pig. But he offered no more arguments.

"Mmm," Buster said mysteriously as he studied him.

"Mmm," the others agreed.

And that was the extent of the conversation for another long minute before Buster finally stirred on the stool, snapped his fingers, and called in his piping voice, "Chuck, are we still carrying that tramp tux outfit from last season?"

"We got it. Top hat, tails, the whole bit."

"What are you going to do to me?" Craig demanded.

"Should fit him, too, with a little pinning here and there."

"Perfect. We'll go with the lovelorn-tramp shtick. Give it a twist, though. Make him a bridegroom jilted at the altar by his ladylove."

"That's genius, Buster."

"What are you going to do to me?" Craig demanded.

"We'll need the wilted bridal bouquet, the oversized brass wedding ring and the mock wedding license out of props."

"No problem. They're there."

"What are you going to do to me?" Craig demanded again.

"Patience," Gloria scolded, leaning over him. "We're going to make you over into a proper joey."

"Joey? I don't want to be a—"

"Relax. That's just circus slang for a clown."

What had been strained silence was suddenly noise and action as they attacked him from all sides with costume and makeup. Craig squirmed in alarm, struggling with the urge to fight them off and bolt from the van.

Gloria, taking pity on his nerves, decided to instruct Craig in clown lore. It didn't take his mind off the ordeal, but he tried to listen politely while they worked on him.

"Now," she said brightly, "we're not going to do anything extreme to you, so don't get anxious. Tramps never use the elaborate makeup. But if you're going to be one of us today, you should know about clowns. Because most people think a clown is a clown, but that's just not so. There are really several basic categories." She ticked them off on her fingers. "You got your classic whiteface with his jolly face and pompoms. You got your august with his darker hobo looks. And you got your rube. Rube is essentially what Rachel is being in the first part of her Pete Jenkins routine."

"Don't forget the carpet clown who does the walk-arounds between acts," her husband reminded her.

"Chuck, that's not technically a separate division. Oh, and don't worry about needing any dialogue. Of course, the earliest clowns *were* talking clowns. Sort of a version of to-day's stand-up comedians. But now we rely completely on pantomime. Yours will be fairly simple for this gag. Buster, don't you think he could use a little more liner down around the eyes and mouth to give him that really sad, hangdog look?"

They painted him, they equipped him, they directed him.

"We're giving you an Emmett Kelly image," Buster said, "because you'll be doing an Emmett Kelly bit. Of course, it's against clown code to ever copy another clown's face or his material. But Emmett's gone now, and I don't think he'd mind us borrowing his look for one afternoon."

"You're going to be a different person altogether in that ring," Chuck advised. "Just forget who you are and go with it."

"You'd better repeat the routine back to us," Gloria said, "so we're sure you've got it."

In bewilderment, Craig endured their preparations, listening, nodding, mumbling. And hating it all. When they were done with him, they propped a big mirror in front of his face. He found himself gazing in shock at a tragic mask under a scraggly black wig—a bulbous-nosed, unshaven creature with unhappy eyes and great mournful mouth. He looked like a fool. He *felt* like a fool.

Craig slouched on the trunk, moaning in defeat. "If Rachel doesn't kill me first, she's going to laugh her head off. They're all going to laugh at me."

Felix, chortling, stuck his face down into Craig's. "That's the whole point, Hollister. That's *just* the whole point."

He couldn't do it. It was a mistake. He felt sick. He felt degraded. He felt as though he was about to walk into a huge disaster.

A nerve-racking eternity later, the disaster had swallowed him up as he stood quaking in baggy tux and floppy shoes outside the back door to the big top. He heard the band inside the tent playing the lively music for Rachel's riding act. He heard the noise of the crowd packed into the stands. He wanted to throw up. He wanted to pass out. He wanted to run away. He couldn't run away. Word had spread, and the whole company was pushing up gleefully behind him, hoping to watch the fun.

Felix was on one side of him, Buster on the other. They were hanging on to him, waiting for just the right moment to launch him. Gloria, peeping through the back door curtain, was holding her hand up, ready to signal them. Her hand dropped. "Now," she said.

Craig felt himself shoved through the curtain, found himself stumbling down the entrance aisle. The brassy music crashed inside his head, the spotlights blinded him, a sea of unfriendly faces gaped at him.

It was a nightmare. He was a tough ex-marine. He was a conservative bank's sober-minded representative. He was about to embarrass both the marines and the bank. He was about to make a humiliating spectacle of himself. Why? Why was he doing it?

The answer that came to him was sudden, obvious and simple. He needed to woo and win the woman he loved. And for that, prouder men had braved every variety of horror known to humanity. He guessed he could endure this particular one. Well, hell, he could face anything for Rachel.

The realization gave Craig all the courage he needed. Drawing a deep breath, squaring his shoulders, he marched the rest of the way along the player's aisle and into the glare of the ring.

Rachel had suspected nothing. She'd been busy with her own complicated preparations before the show and hadn't gone near clown alley. Nor had anyone on the lot permitted her to learn what was happening.

Now, concentrating on her performance with Warrior, she wasn't aware of the presence of the strange clown at the edge of the ring. She was at that stage in her routine when, bumpkin garb shed to reveal her femininity in the glittering tights, she circled the ring on Warrior's back. This was the serious part of her program and she was struggling to maintain a crispness and an energy for each difficult feat. Not easy when her spirits had been rock-bottom low since her parting earlier from Craig. She had been so wretched that she had longed to cancel her act. But, of course, that was unthinkable.

Her first clue that something was wrong was when she heard a wave of titters from the audience. Why were they laughing? They weren't supposed to be laughing at this point in the routine. Then as the chestnut Arab swept her around the ring, out of the corner of her eye, she caught a glimpse of the woebegone clown who had invaded her spotlight.

His presence startled her, destroyed her precise timing. The giggling stands were no longer watching her. They were watching this idiot in a tramp bridegroom outfit as he bent over with a whisk broom, carefully dusting the surface of the ring curb. From his top hat, he produced an oversize wedding license, an enormous wedding ring and a wilted bridal bouquet, spreading them out along the flat ring curb.

Who was this character? This wasn't a Donelli clown. What was he doing in the ring, and where was Ray? Why wasn't her ringmaster removing him?

Her gaze went frantically to the back door, then to the front door. The whole company was there, jamming both openings. Her eyes pleaded for someone, anyone, to come to her rescue, but her people blithely ignored her appeal.

This was crazy! What was going on?

She was in no mood to continue, but years of training and tradition had taught her to preserve her performance at all costs. She struggled on with her act, even though she had completely lost her audience. They were howling at him now. Howling at this jerk who was hunkered down on the ring curb with his bouquet, his license and his ring as he stared with tender, unwavering longing at the object of his desire. Her.

It was one of the oldest gags in the business, a simple, highly effective upstaging. And it still worked.

Rachel was incensed. Outraged. She could no longer ignore the brazen interruption. Bringing Warrior to a standstill, she leapt cleanly from his back and headed for the ringside. There was a stage smile on her face, but her green eyes were flashing with indignation as she confronted the tramp clown placidly waiting for her on the ring curb.

"I don't know who you are and what you think you're doing," she muttered through clenched teeth, "but you're lousing up my act, and if you don't—*Oh, no!*"

Close up, she recognized him. She didn't believe what she was seeing under the silly wig and the even sillier makeup, but she recognized him.

Smothering a gasp, Rachel leaned over him, hissing an angry, "Who put you up to this? Felix, I bet! I'll kill him! You look ridiculous!"

"The crowd doesn't think so," Craig answered her casually. "They think I'm pretty amusing."

Chuck and the others had been right, he thought. Something magical had occurred when he'd entered the ring. He'd been swept up into the spirit of the gag, his broad humor instantly invoking audience empathy. He was actually enjoying himself.

Catching up the drooping bridal bouquet, Craig got to his feet, sketched a courtly bow and offered her the artificial flowers. "Smile sweetly, Rachel, and take the flowers. They're watching us."

She wanted to poke the bouquet into his false nose, but for the benefit of the crowd, she dropped a curtsy and accepted the flowers. She went on smiling, he went on looking mournful and the band went on playing, drowning their whispered exchange. No one in the stands was fooled by the cover-up, though. They seemed to sense exactly what was happening and were fascinated by the proceedings, waiting to see just how it was all going to turn out.

"All right," she ordered him, "you've had your little joke. Please leave the ring and let me finish my act."

Craig answered her by picking up the prop wedding license and waving it beseechingly in her face.

She pushed the license away with a fierce, "Why are you doing this? Never mind. Whatever it is, it won't work. You put me out of your life, now I'm putting you out of mine. *Get out of my tent, Hollister!*"

"You can't throw me out," he informed her serenely. "It's not your tent. It's my tent." Leaning forward, he plucked the bill of sale out of the bridal bouquet where he had earlier tucked it. He held the receipt under her nose. "See, it wasn't a donation from Miller and Hodge. I paid for the canvas myself."

Her look of dismay almost caused him to drop his character and grin outrageously. Instead, he consoled her with a gentle, "Aw, don't worry, Rachel. It's not charity. I'm counting on you paying me back in easy installments. Say, over the next forty or fifty years?"

She suddenly couldn't think, didn't know how to answer him.

"I plan to stick real close," he promised her. "Plan to be right there to see to it that you make those payments."

"Craig, please, you can't— What are you doing? *No, don't!*"

The lovesick clown was ignoring her panic. Scooping up the last of his props, the oversize wedding ring, he dropped to one knee on the floor of the ring.

"This is a proposal, Rachel," he said, holding the symbolic ring out to her in an attitude of prayer. "A marriage proposal. The audience understands it. Why can't you understand it?"

"Craig, don't do this!" she begged him desperately. "You're making fools out of both of us! Get up! Oh, please, get up!"

"I'll get off my knees as soon as you agree to marry me."

Rachel had never been self-conscious in front of her audiences. Until now. She was embarrassingly aware of the watching crowd, their gazes swinging from his face to hers and back again, like spectators at a breathless tennis match.

Even the band had stopped playing to gape at the comic scene.

"You know you don't mean it," she pleaded with him.

"Now, why would I be down here like this if I didn't mean it? Come on, Rachel, I won't let you throw me out of the tent, and I won't let you throw me out of your life."

"You don't want to be in my life. Not like I need you to be there."

"Think again. Because that's what I did after you walked out of the trailer. I thought about it again. I want it, Rachel. I want it badly. Marriage, kids, all of it."

There was a hush now throughout the big top. The tension was finally shattered by a portly man on the front bleachers hollering, "For heaven sakes, girlie, say yes so we can get to the elephants!"

The crowd roared in mirthful agreement.

"Listen to them," Craig demanded. "They know what they're talking about, Rachel. Come on, how can you ever have marriage or kids with anyone but me?"

That was just it, she realized helplessly. She couldn't!

She understood him then. *He meant it!* He actually meant it! He was ready to want what she wanted, the commitment of marriage and children. How could he not mean it when he was kneeling there in that absurd clown getup, sacrificing his pride and dignity, risking the ridicule of a mob of strangers in order to convince her that they belonged together?

"Husband and wife?" he implored with his woeful tramp face.

Her heart leapt. He was something he hadn't been before. He was wild and wonderful, and she could no longer resist him. This time, her trembling smile was genuine. "Put the ring on my finger," she told him.

Spoiling his sorrowful image with a jubilant grin, he snapped to his feet and reached for her hand. The stage ring was much too large for one finger. He ended up pressing it over two fingers at once.

The crowd burst into exuberant applause when the clown rapturously kissed the lady bareback rider.

"So, are you going to tell them?" Craig asked her eagerly as she nestled in his arms inside the snug, private world of her trailer.

Rachel stirred at his side on the sofa, lifting her puzzled gaze to his. "Tell who what?"

"Our grandchildren—that their grandfather went into the ring as a circus clown to persuade their grandmother to marry him."

One of his tawny, quirking eyebrows was arched inquisitively as he gazed down at her, waiting for her answer. She loved those expressive eyebrows. Come to think of it, there wasn't anything about him that she didn't love. Reaching up a forefinger, she began smoothing the eyebrow. "You're awfully smug about that, aren't you?"

He caught her finger, pressing it to his mouth in a lingering kiss. "Yeah, I thought I made a pretty good clown."

Rachel laughed. "I'll make a deal with you. I'll tell the story if you promise never to go into the ring again."

He dropped her finger, looking boyishly injured. "You don't think that I made a good clown?"

"Mmm, let's just say that I think you make a much better financial troubleshooter."

"That, too," he agreed. He frowned. "The way I see it, I've got a choice to make here. Either I retire from the ring and resume my career with the bank, or I enroll in a good clown school somewhere." He cocked his head to one side, thinking about it. "Naw, I guess it'll have to be the bank."

"Wise choice."

"Only if you're ready to leave the road and join me. There must be a veterinary practice somewhere in the St. Louis area just waiting for you."

"One with facilities large enough to accommodate elephants," she insisted. "Because winter quarters isn't that far away from St. Louis, and someone has to look out for the animals in the off season."

"Who else? Besides which, we'll want to be close enough to the circus to make sure we don't get left out of any family celebrations in the cookhouse."

"Right." It was her turn to frown. "Small problem."

"What?"

"Since I'm going to be busy in St. Louis practicing veterinary medicine and having those babies who'll be the parents of the grandchildren waiting for your clown story, then..."

"Yes?"

"Well, who's going to take the show out on the road?"

"Got it figured. We monitor the circus from home while Felix and Ray manage it on the road. Bet they'll do it."

"I'll bet they will, too."

"Sure. At least until we get one of our kids old enough to take control of the show."

"Think any of them would be interested in doing that?"

"Bound to be at least one. Circus blood, remember?"

Rachel's head went down onto his shoulder, her manner sobering as reality intruded on the dream. "Craig, are we being serious here about any of this?"

His arm tightened around her reproachfully. "Sure, we are. Under all the fun, we're being totally serious about every bit of it."

She nodded slowly. "Then we have to realize that after this season, there may no longer be a Donelli's Circus for any of this to happen."

"Who says?"

"Darling, be practical."

"I am being practical. That's my business, in case you've forgotten. Rachel, we are going to preserve the show. We'll do it."

"How?"

"By implementing those changes I recommended. By modernizing the show."

"Tell me," she implored, needing to be assured that it was possible.

He described for her the changes he wanted for Donelli's, the additions he was convinced would make the show profitable. "Like I said before, we'll blend some high-tech acts with the traditional ones on the program. Move into a sturdier big top. Maybe have mechanized seat wagons. Install computers for our office operations. And cellular phones. I want phones in all of the vehicles so that we have efficient communication to cover any emergency."

She began to share his excitement. "What else?"

"I've been thinking about a sideshow. The old circuses always carried sideshows."

Rachel was alarmed by the suggestion. "You don't mean curiosities and freaks, because Donelli's has never—"

"Not that kind of sideshow. An updated version of the concept. Something featuring electronic marvels, psychic phenomenon displays, the latest video games. That kind of thing. The stuff that young people go for. Think of the potential here, Rachel."

"Yes," she said, responding to his enthusiasm, "it sounds good to me. It sounds like it could attract a big traffic, all of it. I can see that now. But, oh, Craig, the money! It would cost a lot of money, and the bank would never—"

"Trust me," he said firmly. "The money is already there. Enough of it, anyway."

She pulled back from his embrace in order to fully see his face. There was a slight note of grimness in his expression. It worried her. "What money? I don't understand."

He hesitated, then made himself tell her. It was important that they keep no more secrets from each other. "The same money that I dipped into to buy the replacement big top. It—it's insurance money, Rachel. Lynn and I both carried large policies. I didn't think it was the best way of investing funds, but she was stubborn about it. She wanted to be sure that there was plenty of money to raise David in case anything happened to one or both of us. Of course, we never dreamed that David would—'' He paused to swallow the emotional lump in his throat, then went on. "Anyway, I couldn't bring myself to touch it afterwards. I didn't want to remember it was even there.''

"Craig—''

"No!'' He put a finger over her lips, silencing her. "Don't say it. I want it this way. It's time to use that money, put it to work for something worthwhile. I think Lynn would have liked that.''

Craig pulled her back into his arms, his voice brightening again. "So, no objections. It's my circus now, too, remember. Well, the big top is, anyway.''

"Partners,'' she said softly. "I like the sound of that.''

"Yeah,'' he agreed, drawing her over his hard thighs to settle her possessively on his lap, "it's kind of satisfying, isn't it?'' He began nuzzling her throat, his voice husky. "I love you, you know.''

Rachel wilted against him with a long sigh. "I do know. You told me this morning. Just before I thought I was losing you.''

"Now, how could you possibly lose me?'' he wondered aloud, pausing to gently nibble her ear lobe. "I wouldn't have let that happen. Not when I've found the other half that makes me whole.''

"It almost happened, though,'' she reminded him, her hand lovingly shaping his strong jawline. "And I never want to live through that kind of fear again. But—''

"What, sweetheart?'' he asked, taking her hand to press a kiss into her palm. "Tell me.''

"I worry a little,'' she said. "The things you said to me this morning about your own fears, and then what you told me in the ring...well, doubts just don't magically vanish like that."

"No," he admitted, "they don't entirely. But I know now that I can handle them. As long as I have you with me, always with me, I can do anything." He drew back to gaze directly into her eyes. "Say it, Rachel," he commanded. "Tell me what we told each other this morning. Only this time, not in anger. This time, make it count."

"I love you," she whispered with a deep, slow sincerity that came from her soul. "I love you, Craig Hollister."

"I'll need to hear that a lot," he said, his voice gruff with emotion. "I'll need to hear it all the time."

"Through our children and our grandchildren," she promised him.

"And great-grandchildren," he demanded.

"Always," she guaranteed, her hand stroking his lean, eager face. "Always."

Epilogue

The Reverend Cole addressed the large company of friends and family inside the big top, his voice clear, his manner warm.

"In my long ministry, I've had occasion to perform weddings in some very unique situations. But never before have I had the honor of officiating a ceremony in the center of a circus ring. I've been assured, however, that for the young couple standing in front of me, there can be no more appropriate spot in which to pledge their vows. Looking at their faces now, and at the faces of all of you in the stands who have gathered to share their joy, I don't doubt it for a moment."

The Reverend Cole paused, allowing himself a few seconds to admire the scene. He had never seen a church interior more beautifully dressed for a wedding.

The ring curb had been bound in gold ribbon and surmounted by enormous bows of the same golden ribbon. Banks of flowers were massed on all sides, perfuming the air with their delicate fragrances. The smartly uniformed circus band had played the traditional wedding march for the bride's entrance under the glowing spotlights.

The face of the bridegroom briefly captured the minister's attention. He was an extraordinarily handsome man. But the Reverend Cole realized this was something that went beyond mere physical looks. It was more the result of the proud, loving light that shone in his blue eyes as he gazed at the woman beside him.

All brides are radiant, the minister thought. But this one was exceptionally radiant in a Victorian-style gown of shimmering ivory satin with mutton sleeves and a high, lacy collar, her dark hair crowned with a headpiece delicately wrought in seed pearls. Yes, very exceptional.

This was a couple who would always be happy together, who would never take each other for granted. The Reverend Cole felt this strongly, and he was seldom wrong about the people he married. It was time to unite them.

"Rachel and Craig, will you join hands and repeat after me..."

Felix, who had given Rachel away and who stood now just behind the couple, grinned his approval as the vows were exchanged. Lucille, one of Rachel's attendants, found herself growing misty eyed after she had promised herself she wouldn't let that happen. Molly, Rachel's other attendant, held the bridal bouquet in a hand that trembled with gladness. The creamy roses were real this time. So, too, was the wide, gold wedding band that Hank Sutherland, Craig's best man, offered to the groom a moment later.

When the ring had been placed on Rachel's finger, just as she had placed a similar band on Craig's finger, and when Craig had kissed her with more ardent longing than the Reverend Cole usually observed after his pronouncements, the minister asked the couple to face the crowded stands.

"Ladies and gentlemen," he said, "it gives me great pleasure to introduce you to Mr. and Mrs. Craig Hollister."

Enthusiastic applause shook the canvas of the big top. The Reverend Cole considered it a very memorable ceremony.

At the noisy, festive reception in the cookhouse tent afterward, Craig pressed his mouth to Rachel's ear, whispering a reverent, "Mr. and Mrs. Craig Hollister. I knew it was for real when he said that."

Rachel smiled, her hand blissfully closing over his. "For real and for all time, darling."

"Yes, Mrs. Hollister," he promised happily, "for all time."

Craig gazed at his bride, then at their circus family packed around the long tables. Something inside him swelled with a sensation of completeness. He had been resurrected because of them and because of this woman beside him, whom he so deeply loved. They had given him what he had been denied most of his life, and he would never stop treasuring it. He had finally come home.

* * * * *

NORA ROBERTS

Love has a language all its own, and for centuries, flowers have symbolized love's finest expression. Discover the language of flowers—and love—in this romantic collection of 48 favorite books by bestselling author Nora Roberts.

Starting in February 1992, two titles will be available each month at your favorite retail outlet.

In February, look for:

Irish Thoroughbred, Volume #1
The Law Is A Lady, Volume #2

Collect all 48 titles and become fluent in the Language of Love.

LOL192

THE LANGUAGE of LOVE

Silhouette Special Edition

salutes

MOMENTS OF GLORY

from Lindsay McKenna

In a country torn with conflict, in a time of bitter passions, these brave men and women wage a war against all odds . . . and a timeless battle for honor, for fleeting moments of glory, for the promise of enduring love.

February: RIDE THE TIGER (#721) Survivor Dany Villard is wise to the love-'em-and-leave-'em ways of war, but wounded hero Gib Ramsey swears she's captured his heart . . . forever.

March: ONE MAN'S WAR (#727) The war raging inside brash and bold Captain Pete Mallory threatens to destroy him, until Tess Ramsey's tender love guides him toward peace.

April: OFF LIMITS (#733) Soft-spoken Marine Jim McKenzie saved Alexandra Vance's life in Vietnam; now he needs her love to save his honor. . . .

SEMG-1

Take 4 bestselling love stories FREE
Plus get a FREE surprise gift!

Coming in February from

SILHOUETTE® Desire™

MAN OF THE MONTH

THE BLACK SHEEP
by Laura Leone

Man of the Month Roe Hunter
wanted nothing to do with
free-spirited Gingie Potter.

Yet beneath her funky fashions
was a woman's heart—and body—
he couldn't ignore.

You met Gingie in
Silhouette Desire #507
A WILDER NAME
also by Laura Leone
Now she's back.

SDBL